MARKED FOR DEATH

A DI SCOTT BAKER CRIME THRILLER

JAY NADAL

INKUBATOR
BOOKS

Published by Inkubator Books
www.inkubatorbooks.com

ISBN (eBook): 978-1-83756-177-3
ISBN (Paperback): 978-1-83756-178-0
ISBN (Hardcover): 978-1-83756-179-7

Previously published by the author as Missing.

1

Fuelled by rage, his heart pounded in his chest. Plumes of vapour spewed from his mouth and hung in the stagnant air. His skin tingled with excitement as satisfaction flowed through him. She'd been silenced once and for all.

A vast blanket of white fog hung heavy over the hills. It suffocated every tree, swallowed every distant object. Creeping with a billowy grace and tiptoeing silently around him, it swooped in and skirted the trees. Like a giant eraser moving indiscriminately, the fog eradicated the existing terrain and morphed it into something new. As he stood in a chilly pocket, winter crept into the fabric of his clothes.

He hadn't planned or expected to be swamped by a sea of fog, but his envelopment came with good and bad news. The good was that no one else would be foolish enough to venture this far out of town and the dense blanket provided minimal risk of being discovered or seen. The bad news was he'd have to find his way back to town slowly and run the risk of crashing or hitting an obstacle.

He glanced down at her body, knowing she, too, was swallowed, erased, and eradicated by the whiteness. A shiver of bliss snaked up his spine. Taking one last look at her, he smiled before hiding her body.

With time a worthy opponent and the weather closing in, he searched around and gathered up his belongings. The cold chewed on his face as moisture in the air formed droplets on the end of his nose. He needed to hurry.

Finding his car, he drove off. The smudged, red tail lights of his car disappeared into the white blanket of the night.

HER LIPS WERE NOW cold and moist, oblivious to the chill that surrounded them. Ever so slightly parted in her last moment of expression. Earth and leaf matter filled her mouth from when she had struggled. It clogged her nostrils, her ears and covered her face, like a grotesque mud mask. A face perfectly protected from the inclement weather that accompanied her tonight.

SHE'D TRIED to look her best for when she'd dropped off her kids at Jackie's. Jackie had done her hair for her. Intricate waves, and bounce and body were the terms Jackie had thrown about as she'd pulled, tugged and lifted the brush through her hair.

She'd made the effort of buying a new outfit. A daringly short silver skirt that clung to her milky-white thighs, a white long-sleeved top, matching red underwear, and black-patent peep-toe heels. She'd cooed over the ankle strap fastening and slim four-inch stiletto heel. She'd felt sexy and vibrant rather than slutty or common.

She didn't want to scare him off on their first date. With two kids, stretch marks and a limited budget, she'd done well to look after herself. As much as she wanted to go to the gym and work out, organised fitness was not compatible with her busy life. Her current means didn't allow for dreamy luxuries.

Pausing in front of the mirror, she gave her naked form a look, turning left then right to examine her side profile, pulling on her small bingo wings, pushing up her saggy breasts, and rubbing a hand over the small rolls of fat on her stomach. She convinced herself that if she sucked in hard enough, she could pull it off and give any twenty-five-year-old a run for her money.

Running around in Primark jeans and a T-shirt wasn't the first impression she wanted to give. After a long soak in the bath, she had shaved her legs and treated herself to a Brazilian. She then painted her toenails and fingernails deep metallic red to match her new underwear.

THOSE TOES she'd painted with such care and pride were now, along with her legs, shrouded in a thin layer of cold, wet soil and a dusting of leaves serving as nature's blanket.

Her body cooled rapidly in the chilly winter night, her fingers and toes freezing as the temperature dipped into low single digits.

He dropped down a gear as he descended the long decline into town. He had thrown the last of her belongings out of the window. As much as he wanted to keep them as morbid souvenirs, the risk of being stopped and questioned by the police presented a greater risk. With the thick fog creeping across the outskirts of town, inching its way towards the seafront, there wouldn't be many more cars to pass this way until the morning.

2

Scott thought of a dozen places he'd rather be on a Sunday night than surrounded by two hundred and fifty people at a charity event hosted by Brighton and Hove Council. They'd invited anyone and everyone who had the slightest level of influence or importance.

The guest list included Scott and Cara as police and medical representatives, alongside Meadows and CC Lennon. The group rubbed shoulders with civic representatives, industry leaders, and other charity representatives. The event itself wasn't bad, but it was tedious to spend the evening making polite conversation, and offering obligatory smiles and handshakes to people he had never met and probably wouldn't meet again.

The council were launching a new initiative to tackle the homeless crisis, which everyone knew was a big problem in Brighton. The streets were home to dozens of homeless people who congregated in and around the Royal Pavilion, Pavilion Gardens and under the pier. Drink and drug problems were common amongst most of those who lived rough.

Even though the council continued to tackle the issue, they had also gone to a large expense to host this lavish evening. Scott shook his head at the obvious irony. No expense had been spared with the four-course meal and the string quartet ensconced in one corner. Waitresses delicately balanced trays of free wine as they weaved amongst the crowd, offering anyone who took the time to look at them a courteous and well-practised smile.

Scott glanced around the event hall and admired the ornate architecture. It had been the Prince Regent's riding house once, and little alteration had taken place other than extra lighting added and the gravel floor replaced with wood in 1867. Towards the end of the 19th century, the building had been turned into an archaeological and geological museum. It had adopted a new function as a unique and versatile venue with a magnificent single-span arched ceiling, and a lovingly restored and refurbished sprung maple floor.

"You're not enjoying it, are you?" Scott asked his date.

Cara pursed her lips then gave him the best smile she could. "It's a nice place and a worthy event, but I can't stand the falseness. Besides, I can tell that you're not enjoying it either."

Scott was about to reply when some unknown council executive piped up over the PA system to continue with the speeches after having taken a short break. Scott waited for a lull in the man's droning voice before he continued.

"No, I'm not enjoying it. I think it's a load of hypocritical shit to be honest. They would have been better off using this money to give the homeless a meal and a place to sleep for the night." He placed his arm around Cara's waist. "The only good thing is that there are a few good-looking women here."

Cara snapped her head in Scott's direction. She narrowed her eyes, giving him a cold, hard stare. Then she leaned forward and stomped on his foot.

Scott winced as the pain raced up his leg. He dragged his foot away and waited for the throbbing in his toes to subside. "And I was about to say, they're all eclipsed by this stunning beauty standing by my side."

Cara shook her head and jabbed her elbow into Scott's side. "You are so full of shit, Scott. It must be all that wine you drank. Did you get that line off the back of a cereal packet?"

"It is true. I only have eyes for you. And right now, I'd much rather take you home and get you out of this." He tugged on the edge of her burgundy, off-the-shoulder fitted dress that draped around her ankles.

"Well, any more wisecracks like that and you'll be sleeping in the spare room, young man. Do I make myself clear?"

Scott bowed his head in mock shame before bringing his eyes up.

They passed the next hour networking. Cara bumped into a senior surgeon she knew from the Sussex County. The drunken grin on the man's face revealed his lecherous thoughts about Cara. The man held out his hand to offer a friendly, firm handshake but lingered longer than she considered polite. His brown eyes glanced over her as he took in her appearance.

It was the way the surgeon said, "That's a gorgeous dress that you're daring to wear this evening. Rather flattering I might say," that disturbed her as much as his eyes lingering on her breasts. She shrugged her shoulders, gracefully accepting the compliment. The man's intimate stare left her wondering if she'd overdone it with the outfit. It was tight and clingy like a second skin, and alluring. But she knew her big-breasted, hourglass figure, long legs, and dark-brown hair cascading over her shoulders made it a dress that suited her.

As hard as she tried to steal herself away from the surgeon, he moved in a drunken stupor around her, blocking off every opportunity to step away from him. Finally, she looked over his shoulder at Scott, and made a silent "come and rescue me" plea.

Scott did and led her over to a small table that he'd found in the corner, away from the many conversations that rumbled and reverberated around this majestic room. They both slumped in their chairs, Scott the worse for wear and Cara desperate to kick off her heels and soothe her aching feet.

"I'm really sorry, Cara," he said as he handed her a soft drink. "I thought we could show our faces, sympathise and agree with the new initiative, grab some free food and drink, and then scarper."

"You hoped that the chief constable wouldn't hang around for long, and as soon as he had shown his face and left, we could do the same."

Scott nodded as he dragged his hands down his face. "Something like that. Even Meadows is still lurking around. Not that it matters. I have to see him at some point."

The room silenced as the leader of Brighton and Hove Council stepped up onto the stage to deliver his keynote speech. He went to great lengths to describe the collaborative relationships that key stakeholders had in delivering this new initiative. He stressed the importance of sharing information and resources to tackle the growing crisis that the town faced.

Although not referring to it, some of his speech stressed the impact of homelessness on the tourism industry. With over eight million visitors a year, tourism pumped around seven hundred million pounds into the local economy. The council had created many initiatives and partnership schemes with more than four hundred businesses to promote the whole city as a visitor destination.

The gathered dignitaries offered a wave of collective nods and rumbles of approval as the leader rattled off more stats and facts. He peered at his audience over the top of his glasses that were perched on the end of his nose. This leader needed their approval. Many businesses represented at the event hosted annual conferences and meetings in Brighton. Such events brought in more than fifty thousand delegates and added a further forty million pounds of economic benefit to the town.

Scott tried to stay awake, as his eyes drifted from one person to another, many with their backs to him. With a shiver of unease, his eyes fixed upon a man who was openly staring back at him. Scott looked away for a few moments before looking back. The man still stared, his hand coiled around the stem of a half-empty wine glass that he held more for effect than anything else. The man appeared oblivious to everything and everyone around him – everyone except Scott. His stare was dark, intent and silently appealing for Scott's attention.

He was an elderly man, dressed in a pristine black tuxedo. His eyes were framed by thick, black glasses, his grey hair combed back, exposing a deep, thickly lined forehead.

Scott dipped his head. "Cara, is it my imagination or am I being watched?"

She glanced over her shoulder at where Scott's eyes were trained. "No, definitely being watched. Do you not recognise him?"

"No, should I?"

"Well something's up, because he's heading over here."

Scott turned to see the man striding over purposefully. An air of authority permeated his stance, with his shoulders pinned back, a measured stride in his pace, and a fixed stare.

"Detective Inspector Baker, I'm Councillor David Levy. I apologise for the interruption. Perhaps I should have introduced myself earlier rather than stand at the back of the crowd and stare at you like some moronic demon."

Scott stood and shook the extended hand on offer. He introduced Cara who remained seated.

"I trust you're both enjoying the evening?" Levy said. Scott nodded pleasantly. "It's always a pleasure when we have the opportunity to meet with key members of the constabulary."

Scott studied the man. He put him around his mid-sixties, maybe older, well-spoken, with a tendency to clip his sentences in a way that made him sound abrupt and cold.

Levy's eyes darted between Scott and Cara. He cleared his throat. "It's not the best time to ask, but I wanted to find out a little more about your procedures in relation to finding missing people."

Any light-headedness Scott had dissipated. He processed the random request, a question he had not been expecting tonight. He'd shed work mode at the door to the hall, and with a few glasses of wine inside him, he now had to give his head a solid shake to jolt it awake.

Levy added, "I appreciate my approach is rather odd, but...I ask this on a personal level. I've thought about whether to approach you all evening and toyed with my thoughts and sanity, if I'm perfectly honest. But I needed Dutch courage" – he waved his half-empty flute glass – "to push myself into approaching you. I just don't know what to do."

The initial air of authority that Levy had melted away with each minute that passed. It was replaced with uncertainty, worry lines, and a furrowed brow. His lips thinned, his eyelids twitched, and his jaw stiffened.

Scott considered the man then offered him a seat at the table.

Levy gave them both a humble nod as he pulled up a seat. He crossed his arms and rested them on the table.

"Can I ask that this conversation be off the record for the time being?"

Scott's eyes narrowed. "Depends why you're asking, Mr Levy."

"Please, call me David." He hesitated for a moment, wrestling with thoughts and worries that clearly tumbled through his mind, looking unsure if he had the courage to continue or if he should leave the table. "It's my daughter – well, one of my two daughters. Rebecca, she's missing."

"I'm sorry to hear that," Scott said. "For how long she has been missing?"

Levy shook his head, his eyes reflecting his agony. "Five years. Well five years and twenty-seven days, to be precise. I want to know more about how you go about locating a missing person."

"Without going into the specifics – as each case is different – we look at who's missing, the circumstances surrounding their disappearance, last known movements, social media profiles, phone records, bank records, and whether they've taken anything like their passport or clothes. And then we often extend our search and speak to their friends for any clues that might suggest why they disappeared. And of course, there are other factors involved –"

"Such as?" Levy interrupted.

Scott paused for a moment. "We look at their medical records for any evidence of mental health issues, the vulnerability and risk profile of the missing person, their personal relationship, and whether they'd been in any trouble recently."

"So rather complex then..." Levy considered, as he stroked his chin.

Scott wondered about the man's motives. If Rebecca had been missing five years, surely the list of investigative tactics had already been exhausted? "It can be. We do what we call a risk assessment of each case, and grade each one as high, medium or low risk, and assign resources accordingly. Some cases are resolved in a matter of hours, others, are..."

Levy stared off into the distance. "Are never solved?"

"Well...cases are left open."

"And that's it? It becomes nothing more than a reference number?"

Though it sounded cold, Levy's assessment paralleled the truth.

"I think you need to understand, David, that thousands of people go missing every year. Over two hundred and fifty thousand people disappear or run away every year in the UK. And some leave for genuine and valid reasons." Scott paused long enough to run a hand down his face. "In Sussex, we don't have the resources to investigate every single missing person's case. That's why we undertake a risk assessment on each one. If they give us a cause for concern, and are not involved in a domestic violence, financial difficulties or relationship problems, then we will do our hardest to investigate them."

"Well, it's none of those," David replied abruptly.

Scott shrugged a shoulder. "Well, not wishing to disagree with you, but we often find that those closest to them don't know all the facts."

Levy shook his head defiantly. "She wouldn't just up and leave. She's had a good upbringing, a happy childhood, and was...is such a cheerful person."

A brief silence followed as both sides weighed up their next reply.

Levy's eyes narrowed. "Would you arrest someone on suspicion?"

"Not without evidence or accusation. And even then we'd do a thorough search. But I'm assuming this was all done at the time of Rebecca's disappearance?"

Levy didn't reply. He gazed into the bottom of his glass.

Scott leant in to make sure he was heard. "At the time, did you feel that someone was involved?"

Levy bowed his head in silence.

"Did you report your concerns to the police?" Scott pushed.

Levy sighed. "No I didn't, but I should have. Is there nothing further you can do?"

Scott exchanged a glance with Cara who'd been a silent spectator throughout.

He said to Levy. "Listen, why don't you come into the station when you have a moment and we can discuss it further, and I can take a fresh statement from you? This isn't the right environment."

Levy nodded in agreement. "I'm sorry for bringing this up on an evening like this, and you are off duty. My apologies."

"Nothing to apologise for. Just understand that if a full investigation had been undertaken five years ago and uncovered nothing, then I can't promise we'll find anything new. Sometimes a missing person is never found."

Levy visibly tensed up before saying, "Inspector, some hope is the only thing that keeps me going."

3

Jackie Cartwright peered through the net curtains for what felt the hundredth time. Weary and tired, she needed sleep. The second she thought about creeping off to her bedroom, little Leo woke, crying. It was that high-pitched, glass-shattering sort of cry that toddlers had mastered. Nature's way of enabling kids to inflict enough torture on their elders to get whatever they wanted.

I'd rather suck concrete through a straw than listen to Leo scream, she thought, as she gritted her teeth through the din.

She picked him up and rocked him on her shoulder.

The sound was so shrill, she thought her ears might rupture. "Well, it's not going to work. He's not my kid and I'm going to bed soon," she muttered under her breath.

She didn't begrudge her friend, Linda, having a good time and had willingly agreed to babysit her children. Naïvely, she had expected it to be a quiet evening where she put the children to bed and settled in front of the TV with a cheap bottle of wine from the corner store.

With the child on her shoulder, Jackie peered out the window at the darkness of the street. At this time of night, only nocturnal animals roamed the streets. A veil of white mist crept through the air, signifying a drop in temperature. She hoped Linda would be home soon.

Their houses stood at the end of the cul-de-sac, Linda's at ninety degrees to hers. From her window, Jackie could see no sign of life at her friend's house. There was no car in the drive, and only blackness in the windows that looked like the thick velvet curtains of the theatre.

"You go for it, girl; you must be having a good time. I bet you've gone back to his place for a good fucking." Her laugh was drowned out by little Leo's painful screams. "Yeah, yeah. I know you want your mum, but fuck it, she isn't here." She added, rubbing his back, "She'll be back soon."

Linda had promised she wouldn't be back late. But Jackie had heard that many times, and sometimes not seen her until the following morning, looking decidedly worse for wear and with a satisfied grin.

Her thoughts turned to Leo and his big sister Shannon. Being lumbered with her friend's kids at short notice meant that she had no food in for them. All she could offer for breakfast tomorrow morning would be cornflakes and milk, and that would have to do. She had things to do, places to be, and couldn't hang around all day being a glorified babysitter.

Leo's cries softened as his exhausted body succumbed to sleep. His mouth hung open, drool dribbling from the corner, his head resting to one side on Jackie's shoulder.

Still no sign.

She laid him down on the sofa and wrapped him in a blanket. With money tight, she couldn't afford to put on the central heating for more than a few hours every evening. His plump red-cheeked face was hot to touch, his hands clammy and sweaty from his incessant crying.

Jackie took a long slow gulp of chilled wine and felt it soothe her tight body and shoulders. Her nerves were frayed, her ears still ringing from Leo's crying. They all had a tough life around here, single mums aplenty, jobs a few. They lived from week to week, not knowing where their next pay cheque would come from. For some like Linda, there was the security of a job in a local supermarket, or a call centre, where staff turnover was high, hours long and pay was just enough to live on.

Jackie's eyes grew heavy and she succumbed to sleep.

HER BODY SHIVERED in the dark, sending a violent chill down her spine. Light reached neither wall nor floor, confining her vision to a small circle of flickering orange, cast by a battery-operated lamp. Inky-black water sloshed below where the rats scurried through the tiny drainage channels that criss-crossed in the darkness.

With just a sleeping bag and a few scraps of food to her name, this had been her home for the past few hours – or perhaps longer, she couldn't be sure. She perched precariously on the crescent-shaped metal ledge, unable to move. A thick metal cable wrapped around her neck was secured to the bottom of some metal steps above her. There was nowhere she could go. She was unsure how far the shaft descended, and the bottom of the extendable steps was too high for her to reach.

It smelt of damp and decay, and now she had added her own bodily waste to the smell.

Despite the cold, she felt the sweat drench her skin. Fear tortured her, churning her stomach, turning into cramps. Fear engulfed her consciousness, pushing all other thoughts aside. Fear tightened her so much, she couldn't breathe; it felt as if someone had their steely hands wrapped around her neck. Her heart raced, and all she wanted to do was curl up into a ball and wait for someone to save her.

But no one would. Who would find her here?

She would die in this godforsaken place. Alone.

A choked cry for help bubbled up her throat, and she felt a tear run down her cheek.

Desolation overcame her as she contemplated this cold, agonising end to her existence.

4

There's a kind of tired that only a good night's sleep could fix, and another that needed so much more. For Jackie, one turned into the other, became like a heavy jacket pushing down hard on her shoulders.

Her leaden eyes snapped open. It was morning. She checked her phone.

No message, no missed call.

She tried Linda's number. A cheerful voicemail greeted her.

For fuck's sake.

She dragged herself over to the window and glared across the road at her friend's house. There was still no sign of movement. The lights were off; the curtains hadn't been moved, and Linda's battered green Corsa was still missing from her drive.

Bolts of anger replaced Jackie's concern; her fingers curled tightly around her phone. There was a limit to her patience. Right now, a five-course, bitter serving of rage was overtaking her compassion. Being taken advantage of occasionally was fine, but this not showing up on time was becoming a regular occurrence for her friend. She had told Linda not to be back too late, and at least drop a text when she was on her way home.

Perhaps her battery ran out of charge? But she could have borrowed someone else's in an emergency. It made no sense to Jackie and now she faced having to get Linda's eldest to school.

Little Leo stirred. Shannon stumbled into the lounge, rubbing her eyes and yawning loudly as she padded across the laminate floor. "Where's my mummy?"

Jackie gritted her teeth in annoyance. She shouldn't have to be dealing with this, and she had a good mind to drop the kids off on Linda's doorstep as punishment for fucking her around. "Mummy just had to pop out again, luv. I'm sure she won't be long, how about I give you some cornflakes for breakfast?"

Shannon didn't answer and flopped down beside Leo, causing him to jerk awake, startled.

"What time will Mummy be back?" the girl said.

Jackie cursed under her breath. She didn't have answers for the kid, and she feared she might regret a few choice words she could offer in reply.

You better fucking turn up soon, Linda. They say men have their brains in their pants; you must've been a man in a former life.

Shannon had her mum's fiery personality. Independent, vocal, and inconsiderate. She was six going on fifteen. Jackie had once witnessed Linda ask Shannon to do something, only for the little girl to turn and walk away, her arms folded, head held high in defiance. The child trod a fine line with her mum, constantly testing her patience, firing one demand after another at her, and expecting Linda to run around after her.

Jackie felt a good old-fashioned clip around the ear would bring the girl back in line. How Linda had the patience she would never know. Perhaps that was why she had been so against having her own children. She had neither the patience nor the maternal instinct.

Shannon scowled. "I'm not going to school without Mummy. She does my hair, and she stops by the sweet shop to buy me a packet of strawberry laces every morning. And then she buys me a packet of chocolate buttons when we come out of school."

"Well, Mummy isn't here, and I'm not into bribery, so you're going to school whether or not you like it."

Shannon stared at Jackie for a moment, uncertainty etched on her face. Her eyes narrowed. "What's bre...bridery?"

"Never you mind, young lady. When you're with me, you have to listen to what I say."

Shannon pulled her knees into her chest, and kicked at Leo's feet in frustration, causing the young boy to cry.

"I'm...not...going...to...school...without...Mummy!"

Jackie scooped up a sobbing Leo and rested him against her shoulder. She swayed him from side to side to pacify the little boy, while his shrill cry pierced her eardrums like a dentist's drill.

"There, there," she offered, as she rubbed his back.

It hadn't crossed her mind until that moment that she would need something special to feed the boy for breakfast. She wasn't sure if he needed baby milk, a jar of baby food, or baby cereal – none of which she had – and Linda had given her none. Things were going from bad to worse, and Jackie was fast running out of options.

"Suit yourself, you silly cow," she said to Shannon. "You can sit here and wait until she comes home. Makes my job a lot easier. I'll get you some breakfast and you can sit quietly. Understand?"

SMALL POCKETS of fog remained as he made the return journey back into town. He regularly drove the same route four or five times a week, which took approximately two hours to complete. Eight miles on the outward leg and the same on the return leg. The going had been harder this morning, with isolated patches of fog and the heavy traffic ahead of him halting every few miles.

His Specialized Allez E5 Elite Red Hook road bike gripped the road well, especially farther up in the hills where the roads were narrow, the bends tight, and two-way traffic a constant hazard. He relied heavily on his Shimano 105 twenty-two speed drivetrain and Tektro Axis Caliper Brakes to give him the pace and the stopping power – a blessing in these wet and cold conditions.

As he picked up speed on the descent, cold licked at his face and crept under his clothes, spreading across his skin like the lacy tide on a frigid winter beach. His thoughts turned to home and taking a warm shower before heading off to work. The weather had turned against him in recent weeks, with icy roads, fog and rain, not to mention an ever-increasing number of potholes.

But there was something he enjoyed about being away from everyone. The freedom to explore and to unburden his mind. Given the choice, he would much rather be on his road bike cycling around the Downs than at home. All he did at home was sit there whilst his wife watched StarPlus, and the Indian version of *Britain's Got Talent*. He would much rather slope off to his garage to do other things.

He leant into a bend and straightened out. Ahead was an obstruction on the road. As he slowed, he noticed it appeared to be nothing more than a discarded pile of rubbish, no doubt thrown from a passing car. But he stopped anyway.

With his bike that weighed one-thousand pounds secured, he stepped out into the road, glancing around before bending down to inspect the items. It appeared to be nothing more than a bag of discarded women's clothes. A wet and muddy silver skirt lay strewn across the road, tyre marks imprinted on the metallic fabric. He pushed it to one side with the tip of his expensive road shoes before peering into the bag.

Time stood still as he fought to catch his breath; his heart hammered against his ribcage in excitement. He felt a twitch and a stirring in his cycle shorts as he reached in and pulled out a black-patent, high-heeled shoe. It was perfectly preserved, dry, untouched, unlike the other half of the pair, which was hidden under the bag. Its heel was broken and scratches tarnished the mirror smooth surface; surface water rain from the road muddied its finish.

He glanced around again, feeling like a naughty schoolboy who had stolen an apple from an apple tree, scared that someone may discover him. His eyes widened with a mixture of intrigue and excitement as he walked the item back to his bike. There, he held the shoe up, marvelling at its design. His thoughts turned to the owner and what she must have looked like tottering around in them. Small, feminine, with her slenderlegs wrapped in that silver skirt that screamed *take me*. With the shoe's peep-toe front, she no doubt had painted toenails.

There were no beauty spots or lay-bys on his route, but he glanced around anyway, wondering what she'd been doing up here.

Was she passing through? Did she have a passionate night with her boyfriend and throw her belongings out of the car for a dare?

With eyes firmly fixed on his new discovery, his hands trembled as he peered inside the shoe. What he discovered sent waves of pleasure through his groin. He needed to get home and hide his new present.

He put the shoe in a small rucksack he carried on his back, placing it with the same precision and care as though it were a rare piece of china.

He rode home quicker than he ever had before.

5

The ache ebbed and flowed like a cold tide, yet the pain was constant. Either Scott had consumed more than he realised or was getting too old to handle much alcohol. He understood at once why they called it a hangover, for it felt as if the blackest of clouds sat over his head with no intention of clearing until late afternoon.

He squinted at the room. His mouth sticky with thick saliva, he groaned before retreating under the duvet, much to Cara's amusement. The hangover felt like a balloon slowly being inflated in his cranium, the pressure mounting.

Scott got up and stumbled to the bathroom. He splashed cold water on his face just to feel something refreshing, and instantly wished he could wash his brain free of the toxins too. The mirror showed his eyes, no longer the bright and alert ones of last night, but bloodshot. Cara's chuckling from the bed reached the bathroom. If he'd been looking for sympathy from her, it was in short supply this morning.

"YOU NEED to come out with me, guv," Mike suggested. "The few sherbets you had last night are nothing compared to what we'd knock back. That would be *proper* drinking."

Scott could offer only the smallest of smiles as he finished the last sticky dregs of his third coffee. "You're not far behind me, Mike; your days of drinking in the army are well behind you. I don't think you would have fared much better."

"You might think that, guv. But cast your mind back to the last pub quiz we went on. Correct me if I'm wrong, but you were drooling like a baby after your fourth pint."

Scott ignored the dig, but he vaguely recalled parts of the inter-departmental, annual pub quiz earlier in the year. If there was one thing Scott hated more than anything else it was losing in a pub quiz. The loss had been harder to bear as it had been to their arch-rivals, Matt's scientific services team.

"Frankly, I'm disappointed that you took Cara and not me," Mike said. "I would have put the council's generosity to far better use. I'm sure I could have got away wearing a dress."

The thought of seeing Mike, with his pot belly and a hairy chest, slopping around in a dress only caused Scott's stomach to lurch.

"There's only three of us this morning," Scott said, moving to a new topic. "Raj is still off with the flu, but I spoke with him yesterday. It sounds like he's at the tail end of it, so I expect him back soon. How are we doing with our current cases?"

Helen's head popped up from behind her PC screen. "I'm

following up an eyewitness account on the Moulsecoomb post office armed robbery. An elderly gentleman, who lives around the corner, has come forward to say that he saw an IC1 male running towards a navy Audi. The vehicle drove off in the direction of Hillside. He could only recall a partial index number and can't be certain of the Audi model, but he says it was big. I'm thinking A4, maybe even A6, but I think the A6 is too big and heavy for a getaway vehicle."

Scott nodded. "Do some preliminaries, but if you don't get far, then park the case to one side. A partial index and a vague description will not get us far. You'd be better off dealing with the stranger rape case. We've got a suspect, and the DNA samples we retrieved from the victim match Marc Abrahams. We need to find him."

Helen flicked through her case file, looking for the information she needed. "We've only got a last known address for him in Preston Park. I've deployed officers to that location twice, but he hasn't been seen for three weeks. I've looked at all his known associates, but I've hit the proverbial wall of silence. He's lying low for sure."

"Are we certain he's still in Brighton?" Scott asked. "Didn't he have connections with South London, Nottingham and Coleraine?"

Helen nodded and shrugged a shoulder. "He does. My next action points are to reach out to local forces in those areas and get them to make enquiries. It's a long shot, but it's possible he's scarpered."

Scott asked Helen to keep him updated before pulling up a seat alongside Mike, to go through his case files. With Mike being more experienced than Helen he had more cases, many of which were complex.

As Helen progressed and grew in experience, Scott

would ensure that she handled more difficult cases to improve her investigative skills base. It was something he had already decided upon following his chat with Abby.

With the difficulties Abby had experienced prior to going on annual leave, he had thought long and hard about how to facilitate her return, and what he could do to make her life easier. It wasn't an ideal solution to have her out of the office, but he had arranged for her to have a work laptop. That would allow flexibility in her shifts, and if necessary, to work from home.

Helen would work closely with DS Abby, so she could take on some of Abby's workload, whilst under Abby's close supervision. More importantly, it wasn't about taking Abby's workload but making her DCs better at their jobs, so less time would be spent supervising and poring over every detail of the jobs they were working on.

Mike took a few moments to give Scott a helicopter view of his current caseload. A violent drug dealer who failed to turn up in court, a spate of commercial burglaries in Hove with the same MO, and a suspicious death of an elderly woman in a care home. Scott went through each case with him, outlining points of interest, and suggesting further actions. Mike had covered most angles already, but Scott needed him to dig deeper for completeness.

Scott glanced at his watch and noticed that his scheduled meeting with DS Meadows had come and gone. By now Meadows would have charged onto the CID floor, tapping the glass face of his own watch to remind Scott. That he hadn't surprised Scott. Meadows had ended up on a table with some heavy drinkers last night, which Scott found ironic considering the nature of the event.

Meadows wasn't much of a drinker, but had drunk far

too much, and was clearly paying the price for it this morning. Scott remembered seeing CC Lennon cast glaring looks in Meadows's direction as the night wore on.

"I had a councillor, David Levy, approach me last night. He asked questions about his daughter. She disappeared over five years ago," Scott said to the team. "Do you remember the case? I don't."

"How many mis per cases do we get? Dozens. What's her name?" Mike asked.

"Rebecca Levy."

He tapped his keyboard and scrolled through the information. He nodded when he found the case file in question.

Scott asked, "We dealt with it?"

"Yup. I remember it now. I was on the case when I was in a different team. DI Harrington was the SIO."

Scott recalled Harrington. He had moved to East Grinstead about two years ago.

"At first Levy wanted to keep it quiet," Mike continued. "Probably because of his position on the council. I think he's also big in the Jewish community and has an active role in the synagogue. At the time I think it worried him what the community might say in case she had just chosen to run away, because he believed in family values."

"And what was the outcome of the investigation?"

Mike scanned through the details on screen. "We did a thorough job of trying to trace Rebecca. Levy might have been quiet about her disappearance out there, but he was very vocal with us."

"Because?"

"He felt we weren't doing enough to locate his daughter. He couldn't believe she would just walk out one day and disappear. He was adamant she was caught on CCTV somewhere."

Scott nodded. "And we followed up all avenues?"

Mike looked at his screen as he relayed further details. They had spoken to friends and family, looked at her medical and banking records, analysed social media profiles, and scoured hundreds of hours of CCTV footage. Despite Levy's reluctance, they had even gone to a press appeal. Other than a few random and inconsequential leads, the appeal had had little impact.

"And what were her last known movements?" Scott asked.

"Well...Levy was prickly about this, but his wife said that Rebecca was going out to buy a new outfit for a date that she had later in the evening. Mrs Levy assumed that she would head into town to do that. We searched hours of CCTV footage along Western Road, and we found nothing to suggest that she was in the area. It was extensive. CCTV footage from observation points along the road and from inside shops. We looked at the main drag along Western Road, The Lanes, and even Hove. It's like she disappeared into thin air."

Scott rubbed his chin as his mind raced. "So, she was abducted soon after leaving home, or went to extreme measures not to be found?"

Mike shrugged, knowing both were definite possibilities. "The fact is we couldn't find anything from her phone records or social media profiles to suggest that she had met anyone new. So, it only deepened the mystery, and our concerns more. At the time we weighed up so many possibilities. Whether she had come to harm? Whether she'd had enough of life in general and decided to pack her bags and leave, destination unknown, or had taken her own life?"

"And what was she like as a person?"

"The usual. Fun loving, liked to drink, going to parties. A typical twenty three year old."

"Was there anything missing from home?" Scott asked.

"Nope. There was a pair of high heels and some red underwear, along with her makeup bag, left on her bed. Her mum assumed that they were in readiness for this date."

"Any names thrown around?"

"No, guv. Why?"

"I can't put my finger on it, to be honest. I got the impression that Levy perhaps knew a little more than he was letting on."

"Well, with no suspect and no reasonable cause for concern, the case didn't go anywhere. Levy didn't like that at all. He felt that we weren't doing enough to find out what happened to her. He was adamant Rebecca wouldn't just up and leave. Her behaviour had given him no cause for concern before her disappearance."

Scott considered the cold case. From the sounds of it, Harrington had done everything possible to locate Rebecca Levy. Whatever was going on in her life, it was clear her parents were unaware. And it was that lack of knowing that was upsetting her father more than anything else. Most parents assumed that they knew their children well. Scott knew from experience that it was rarely the case.

Mike furrowed his brow as he flicked through further pages of notes. "Her medical records indicated that she'd had a termination at nineteen. It horrified the parents when we told them. There was no indication as to the father's identity. We even spoke to her friend, Lexi Freeman."

"And what did Lexi have to say?"

"Rebecca was a happy girl. Sometimes a loner and insecure, but with some drink inside her, she could be a bit of an exhibitionist and, as Lexi put it, a gobby cow."

Scott nodded. "Okay, Mike, thanks for that. I suggested that Mr Levy come in to talk to me, and perhaps we'll look into the case once again. Though after what you've said, I doubt we can do much. I had to say something to pacify him. It sounds as if the initial investigation was thorough. I'd be surprised if we uncover anything new after all these years."

Mike said, "We kept the file open longer than we needed to because of his position, and then closed it. You've got more chance of finding a pube in a sandwich than you have of finding Rebecca Levy."

Scott shook his head at Mike's food remark as he headed off. It did nothing to soothe the waves of nausea that rolled through him.

6

By lunchtime Jackie Cartwright was ready to scream the house down. Shannon had finished the last of the plain digestive biscuits, after moaning incessantly about the distinct lack of crisps, and missed her favourite fruit squash. Where possible Jackie had sat with Shannon, flicking through the kid's channels trying to find something that would settle the girl and keep her occupied for a few hours.

Handling Shannon was the least of her worries. If there was one thing that Jackie hated more than anything else, it was nappies. Despite having changed Leo's nappy occasionally, she still wasn't used to the wave of nausea that hit her every time she opened a soiled one. Her eyes would water, her stomach would heave, and bile would shoot to the back of her throat. She had taken to spraying perfume on a handkerchief and placing it over her mouth and nose, in much the same way that cowboys used to hide their faces in the old western films.

Things were getting serious. She was down to the last

few nappies, a small tub of formula milk, and no spare clothes for the baby. She had tried Linda's phone on the hour, every hour, since this morning. Greeted each time by voicemail. As each hour passed, Jackie's messages had gone from pleasant to concerned, to bordering on abusive.

Linda had not made contact. That niggled in the back of her mind. On past occasions where she had stayed out overnight, she would always send Jackie a text to update her.

If it carried on for much longer, she'd have to do something. What, she wasn't sure. The last thing she wanted was to drop Linda in it with the authorities.

HEAVY RAIN LASHED BRIGHTON. Traffic along the seafront had slowed to a crawl. Drivers stared through windscreens that were being pelted by droplets the size of penny pieces. Cold, driving rain and black menacing clouds robbed Brighton of its zest, and cast a shadowy gloom over the town.

Rain lashed at her lifeless body, washing away the leaves and undergrowth covering her after she'd taken her last breath. Hour by hour speckles of grey flesh sprouted from the dark earth. First her hand showed, then her arm, followed by her thigh, and her shoulder. Her reveal would be complete soon.

COUNCILLOR LEVY LOOKED like a drowned rat as he stood in reception. His collapsible umbrella had offered little in protection against the battering weather in Brighton. Sheets of horizontal rain were sweeping unmercifully across town, soaking those foolish enough to brave it.

Scott stepped through the double doors to the left of reception and extended a hand to Levy. "Mr Levy, thank you for taking up my offer to come in. Let's find somewhere warm where you can dry off."

He looked the man up and down. Levy's wet trousers clung to his legs and the man's rain jacket had rivulets of water dripping from it.

They settled in a quiet corner of the canteen and sipped steaming coffee. A few officers sat farther away, engrossed on their phones or talking in quiet murmurs.

Levy wasted no time. "Did you look into my daughter's case?"

The man's directness was blunt and insistent. A marked contrast to his humbleness at the charity event.

"I have, Mr Levy. I'm more than happy to look into it further when we have the resources to do so, but from what I've reviewed, I believe that the case of your daughter's disappearance was handled thoroughly and professionally. The team involved took all reasonable steps, and all lines of enquiry were followed up meticulously."

Levy stiffened and held Scott's eye. "Inspector, it's been over five years. My wife and I can't accept that she just walked out and disappeared. There must be a fresh appeal for new information. Surely you can stretch to that?"

Scott leant back in his chair and weighed up his options. "Mr Levy are you sure that there's nothing else you can tell me you may have forgotten to reveal, even if it appeared inconsequential at the time?"

Levy narrowed his gaze, his annoyance clear. "Inspector

don't put this on my doorstep. The police have given my daughter's case little due care and attention."

Scott and Levy exchanged a volley of claims and counter-claims that, on occasion, threatened to develop into a full argument. Other officers turned occasionally as their voices grew louder.

"Mr Levy, here's what I suggest," said Scott. "We'll update our missing-persons records online and put out a request for any fresh information. If nothing is forthcoming, then we must accept that unless anything new comes up, the case will remain open."

Levy wasn't happy with the lack of action, but Scott's suggestion appeared to placate the man, if just for the time being.

SCOTT STOOD by his office window, staring at the greyness beyond the glass. The rain slammed against the window. The noise crept into his thoughts as he watched the grey, scraggy clouds roll by. His thoughts turned to Levy's plight and the man's reluctance to accept the fate of his daughter.

He felt sympathy for the man. No parent would willingly accept that their child had walked off or disappeared. Everyone had a reason to disappear – even if it was intentional. Rebecca's case could fall into either camp. She either chose not to be found or someone had taken her against her will. All the evidence pointed to the former. The investigation had been thorough. There was no evidence to suggest kidnapping. And yet, Levy refused to accept the police decision. Levy had been vociferous in his condemnation of how the case had been managed.

With a few weeks left to Christmas, this time carried the most sadness for many families and loved ones. Scott imagined most only had one wish – that the knock on the door, the letter, or the call was to say their child was safe. He hated December. Scott's mind drifted back to a memory of his child Becky helping him wrap her present to Mummy. A sellotape disaster. Scott's face tightened as he glanced at Becky's picture on his desk. Happiness smiled back at him.

Scott's face softened and he smiled. He'd bought Christmas cards for both Tina and Becky. On his next visit to their graves, Cara would be joining him for support. He needed all the help he could get to make it through Christmas and New Year.

Councillor Levy wouldn't have that opportunity, but Scott had already reviewed the case and evidence, if for nothing else than closure for the Levy family.

He flicked off the office light and headed home.

7

Munch coffee shop didn't have the usual calming feel as Scott stirred his coffee, transfixed by the black darkness swirling around the spoon, like a mini whirlpool in a muddied river. Greyness and damp hung in the air following the downpour of yesterday.

Scott couldn't put his finger on it, but he felt out of sorts. Low and jaded. With a moment's peace away from the office, the break gave him an opportunity to process his feelings. And for the first time in many months, he couldn't find an explanation. It was as if all the zing and motivation had leaked out of his pores and sapped him of his drive.

His personal life was going well. Being with Cara had given him the opportunity to love again. To smile, laugh and feel wanted. So, he was certain it wasn't that. His eyes narrowed, and his brow furrowed as he delved into the darkest recesses of his mind, searching for an answer.

Maybe it's a midlife crisis?

He doubted that, but the thought caused him to reflect.

Perhaps it's the job?

He'd been in Brighton for many years now and it was too easy to get stuck in the monotony of routine.

But is now the time to start looking for a new post and starting afresh elsewhere? A new patch? A new set of challenges?

That didn't resonate with him either. He had a good team, a new relationship, and he knew Brighton well.

Are they excuses to avoid change?

It was far too easy to get comfortable with one's surroundings, job, and life. It was why so many people struggled to accept and cope with change. Human beings were creatures of habit. From the minute they got up to the minute they went to bed, their lives were nothing more than a series of automated behaviours that formed their daily routine.

Scott knew that more than anyone else. His study into human behaviour had shown him fear was the common denominator that underpinned every kind of conflict in life. Many fears remained in the unconscious but still gave rise to debilitating emotional conflicts, or lent to unhealthy decision making.

He was falling into a trap where his routine was so embedded in his psyche and daily life that the fear of change outweighed the excitement of change.

The answers he looked for were not in the black coffee that he stared into.

"Penny for your thoughts, Inspector?"

James, one of the staff members in the café pulled him out of his reverie. He was a slim man, with tightly cropped hair, an even tighter T-shirt, and drainpipe jeans that looked as if they had been painted on. He was cleaning away the table beside Scott and giving him a concerned smile.

Scott smiled back and offered James the slightest of

shrugs. "I just needed some peace and quiet away from the office to go through a few things."

James raised both hands, saying, "I know I'm imposing. I'll leave you to it. Give me a shout if you need another refill."

Scott let out the loudest of sighs, which caused a few people to glance around for the source of the interruption to their conversations. Scott chuckled to himself.

His thoughts turned to Abby. She was due back tomorrow, and from all accounts, had enjoyed her stay at the apartment in Spain. She had sent Scott texts daily to begin with, thanking him, and prying to see what everyone was up to in the team. He missed her, more than he dared to admit. She annoyed the hell out of him, with her fuzziness and OCD tendencies, but he missed her as a friend and as a colleague.

Perhaps that's why he'd felt out of sorts for the last few weeks. Abby was part of his familiarity, part of his daily routine, and without her, there was a gap in his life. He hoped – in fact he prayed, that she returned with a clearer state of mind than before she'd left. The threat of her leaving the job hung in the air, but he sensed that his olive branch of a holiday and changes to her working patterns had somehow diminished that risk. He looked forward to seeing her moody features and being on the end of her negativity about everything in life.

His phone vibrated in the chest pocket of his jacket. He whipped it out to see Mike's name on the screen. "Mike, what's up?"

Mike's response was enough to send a surge of electricity through every nerve and cell of his body.

The call had come in less than fifteen minutes ago. A body discovered in a shallow ditch by the side of a road, south of Plumpton. Mike had deployed SOCO and had alerted Cara. Local units had sealed off the area. A shocking discovery had been made by a postal collection driver who was collecting mail from a remote post box by the side of the road.

Scott gathered intelligence regarding the discovery as they headed north out of town. As usual, Mike drove with the care and delicacy of an army tank driver, as he ploughed through town traffic, and then roared onto the Lewes Road.

They speculated on what they would discover as they approached signs for Plumpton and saw the flashing blue lights of a patrol car blocking the entrance to a track that led off the main road. Preliminary reports from the scene had suggested that the victim may have lain undiscovered for a few days. The track was narrow and often used as a cut-through to a neighbouring village, or by farm vehicles, or courting couples.

White scientific services vans were positioned close by, as well as Cara's car. SOCOs in white paper suits, blue foot coveralls, and blue latex gloves constructed the frame for the white tent that would be placed over the body.

Scott and Mike signed the scene log before being directed by a uniformed officer down the track towards the body. The ground underfoot was wet and squelchy. To avoid disturbing the scene any further and to provide a safe route to the scene, forensic officers had laid down metal stepping plates. Scott ran through several scenarios in his mind, as he wondered how long the body had remained exposed to the elements and nocturnal animals.

He and Mike paused by the inner cordon, a boundary blue-and-white tape that marked the area of focus for the forensic officers. Cara, dressed in an identical white paper suit with latex gloves and shoes, knelt beside the victim. From their position as observers, Scott could see the body of a white female lying on her right side. A clear plastic bag over her head had been secured by silver duct tape around her neck. She was naked from the waist down, the grey hue of her flesh streaked with brown mud stains.

"I think we can rule out suicide..." Mike suggested.

"Possibly, but the first rule of investigation, Mike, rule nothing out."

Mike cleared his throat. "Local officers haven't been able to glean anything. The idiots trampled all over the scene. There was no sign of any possessions that would indicate her ID."

The lifeless body transfixed Scott. He thought about the circumstances that would have led to the woman's tragic demise. The area was a known location for courting couples. The victim could have been lured here under the false promise of discreet passion, or she may have been dumped here because of its isolation.

A full thirty minutes passed before Cara squelched over to them, a grim look on her face. Matt Allen, the crime scene manager, joined them. Feeling cold, Scott stomped around on the spot having left his coat back at the office. The chill of the late morning crept under his suit jacket and shirt. He hadn't expected to be standing on a cold, damp, wet morning down a muddy lane.

Cara snapped off her gloves. "I'd say a combination of strangulation and suffocation appears to be the cause of death. There are clear impressions across the front of her neck that would suggest some form of compression."

"Suffocation?"

"Yes, Scott. I would suggest that someone placed the bag over her head whilst she was still alive."

He nodded. "Any other indications to suggest a struggle?"

Cara shook her head. "It's hard to tell, she's caked in mud and dirt. I'll need to clean her up before I can be certain. There isn't any clear evidence of damage to her skin following death. I think the weather saved her in that respect as I can't imagine too many animals wanting to be out here."

"Any indication on time of death?" Mike asked.

Cara grimaced as she shot a look over her shoulder at the gruesome body. "Again, hard to be precise. The weather, external temperature, and the fact it appears she was covered would all be influential factors. There's still primary flaccidity; she's stiff and cold. I would work on a timescale of around thirty-six hours, maximum."

"So that takes us back to Sunday," Scott said. "I can't imagine much happening around here on that day. There may have been a few courting couples along the track. Mike, can you organise for uniformed officers to ask around, and do door to door in the village? We're looking for the usual stuff, unusual activities, and strangers, noises, etcetera."

Mike nodded as he jotted a few lines on his notepad.

Scott turned to the lead SOCO. "Matt, it would be helpful if your team could identify whether the victim was alive and killed *in situ* or dumped here."

"We'll do our best, Scott, but to be honest, this is a dreadful scene to examine her properly. I expect that the rain has washed away most forensic evidence. As for footprints and tyre marks..." Matt shook his head and stared at the ground. "A long shot and we may get lucky. I'm arranging for extra coverings and lights to be sent over. I think the team will be here for a while."

Weather proved to be their main adversary rather than time itself. They would rely on extracting vital forensic evidence from the body. Soil samples taken from the body may help to identify whether they corresponded to the soil profile and composition of the area where the body was found.

"I can fit her in for a post-mortem this afternoon, if that works for you, Scott?" Cara said.

"That works for me. Once SOCO have done their job, we can arrange for her to be moved."

Scott instructed Mike to remain at the scene and left with Cara. Extra officers were being drafted in to assist with the search of the area. It would be a difficult terrain to assess. A mixture of farmland and dense forest made access challenging during the current wet conditions. With further rain forecast over the next twenty-four hours, a sense of urgency rippled through the officers.

8

The bleakness of the day continued long after Scott's visit to Plumpton. He had accompanied Cara and the body to the Lewes Road mortuary. The coldness of the examination room did nothing to warm him after several hours at the crime scene. He stood off to one side of the examination table.

Scott took a moment before Cara started to cast a detailed look at the victim from head to toe. Neil, Cara's assistant, had removed some earth and debris that clung to the woman's skin. It would be examined later for evidence. Scott put the woman in her thirties. Her skin was taut, and her hair, though dirty and caked in mud, suggested it was blonde and shoulder length. He spotted a heart-shaped tattoo on her left hip and requested a close-up photo of it.

The post-mortem began with a careful inspection of the body. Cara weighed and measured the body, noting the cadaver's clothing, as well as valuables and characteristics such as eye colour, hair colour and length, and age.

She then moved on to removing the subject's remaining

clothes before examining the body, searching for any alien deposits, identifying marks such as scars or tattoos, or injuries. She took samples of hair, nails and nail scrapings.

Throughout the examination, Scott watched and observed. Cara moved around the body with grace, precision and tentative care, as she recorded everything discovered both verbally and on a body diagram.

Cara and Neil advanced their examination of the cadaver.

The woman's vital organs were removed, photographed, and weighed. A single incision across the back of the head allowed for the top of the skull to be removed so the brain could be weighed and examined.

"She died of strangulation rather than suffocation," Cara said. "The impressions around her neck are visible. The tissue damage beneath the surface is extensive. Her windpipe collapsed, and my guess is it was because of extreme pressure."

"Would it require the force of a male?" Scott asked.

"More than likely. The collapsing of the windpipe would require some force. My guess is that whoever committed the act used their full upper body strength. You might want to see this as well..." Cara pointed to extensive bruising around the upper arms. "It's almost identical on both arms."

"What would you suggest was the cause?"

"It's an informed guess, but I have seen it before on one other victim. The impressions are like those caused by someone sitting on a person's chest then using their knees to pin the victim's arms to the floor. The victim would be powerless to fight back. That position and that same pressure would correlate with the amount of tissue damage on the neck."

Scott crossed his arms and considered the implications. "And the plastic bag?"

"Again, I would suggest that someone taped the bag over the head moments before strangulation. There is residue inside the bag which suggests that the victim was alive. I've taken swabs to confirm that it belongs to the victim. I'm certain it does."

"Was there a sexual motive involved?"

Cara nodded. She pointed a long metal probe at the woman's pelvic region. "There's extensive bruising to the vaginal opening and the upper thighs. It appears to have been a forceful sexual assault. I doubt it was consensual. There are accompanying bite marks to the front of her left shoulder. I'll arrange for a forensic odontologist to analyse them. It might help you as the case progresses. I've also taken vaginal swabs."

"Anything else of interest?" Scott enquired.

"There is, as a matter of fact. As you can see she has little pubic hair. She is mousy brown in colour. But I retrieved a loose, black pubic hair."

"So that could be the assailant's? Or whoever she last had sex with?"

Cara shrugged, but agreed in principle with the idea.

Scott left Cara to finish the post-mortem and confirmed that he would call later for a complete update.

ON HIS RETURN to the office from the mortuary, Scott tracked down Meadows and gave him an update.

Meadows was keen for Scott to keep a tight rein on the investigation as there had been an alarming increase in sex-related crimes in Sussex and Hove over recent months. Much of it was being blamed on the drugs being peddled in nightclubs and pubs.

Brighton in recent years had become a Mecca for stags and hen dos. Every weekend, large groups would drift in and out of the pubs and clubs. The women wore outlandish outfits, with sashes publicising their celebrations. The men were no better dressed, wearing identical T-shirts announcing they were celebrating the groom's final days as a bachelor.

This influx of partying had led to an increase in stranger rapes, many of which went unreported or unsolved.

Scott and Meadows discussed the possibility of whether this crime had been planned or was a random attack. That the victim was missing her skirt, shoes and underwear only added to the uncertainty regarding the motive for the attack.

The influx of officers to the crime scene, and a subsequent search of the area had given Scott and his team their first breakthrough. A handbag was found a few yards away from the body, discarded behind trees. Inside it were a driving licence, bank card, some keys and a purse containing cash. The contents belonged to Linda Allen, aged thirty-three, from Brighton.

The discovery helped Scott narrow down a possible motive. For the time being, they could rule out robbery. Sixty pounds in cash and a bank card would have been the first items to be stolen.

The bag and its contents were being pored over by a member of Matt's team, searching for any clues that could help them to narrow the search further.

JACKIE CARTWRIGHT HAD all but given up on Linda's return. It had now been two full days since Linda had left her children with her. With the third night approaching, any patience Jackie had was long gone and any concern replaced with anger.

Shannon and Leo were at their wits' end. The pair had alternated from crying and screaming to bouts of silence. Jackie had no answers for Shannon's questions, or no way to soothe Leo who stared at her through sodden eyes. It had crossed her mind to report Linda missing, but she feared it would only cause further complications with the authorities and social services. After the spat that Linda and her mum had had, she doubted that Clare Allen would offer any sympathy or express concern.

"I'll fucking kill her if she's fucked off."

Jackie had given up trying to call Linda's mobile. She had taken a few moments during the quiet moments to race across the road and bang furiously on Linda's door. When no answer was forthcoming, she had pressed her face against the front window, cupping her hands and peering through a small gap in the curtains into the darkened room.

Two nights had gone by and Linda hadn't rung or answered her phone. She wasn't a bad mum; it's just that she sometimes went off the rails.

Jackie wondered what else she could do. Linda had left no keys with her, and she needed to get inside to get new supplies for the kids, as well as search for Linda.

She needed help. As she walked back towards her house, her mind raced with options. There was only one thing left to do.

9

The address on the driving licence took Scott and Helen to a small cul-de-sac just off the Ridgeway in Woodingdean. They pulled up to a row of identical, small bungalows that lined either side of the road. It was a quiet, residential street, and not the best kept. Scott noticed that several of the houses were in dire need of a lick of paint and new windows.

Scott rapped on the door a few times as Helen peered in through the front window. With no answer forthcoming, Scott knocked harder. He grimaced and turned to Helen, who shook her head to confirm that she could see no sign of movement or disturbance. They split, with Scott going one way to check the perimeter of the building, whilst Helen attempted to gain access to the rear garden.

"The side gate is locked, guv," she said. "I can't see anything through the windows. I think no one's at home."

Scott agreed. He'd listened through the letterbox flap and heard nothing. Despite his announcement of police, only silence greeted him.

The pair headed off in different directions, to knock on neighbours' doors and find out if anyone had seen Linda.

The household to the left of Linda's didn't reply, and with an empty driveway, Scott assumed that they were out for the evening.

The next door along was opened by a woman with a phone to her ear, and a young toddler balanced on her hip. Scott introduced himself and explained the reason for his visit. His words appeared to cut her like a shard of glass, leaving her speechless.

"Madam, are you okay?" Her face was ashen, her mouth gaped open. Fear, anxiety and curiosity appeared to collide with a monumental bang.

Jackie Cartwright offered a nervous nod as she swallowed hard. "Yes, yes. I'm fine. Yes, I do know the woman across the road. Linda's my friend. I'm minding her children. What's happened?"

Helen joined Scott at Jackie's front door. Scott asked if they could come in. Jackie stuttered her reply before taking a few steps back and leading them through to the lounge.

Two children stared at the visitors. Their eyes darted between Scott's sombre face and Helen's warming smile. Helen tried to soothe their apprehension. Jackie took the children into the kitchen, giving the older girl a packet of crisps and a carton of Ribena to keep her busy. She strapped the little boy into his pram, leaving him with a soft puzzle book to play with.

Jackie perched on the arm of the brown sofa. She bit her bottom lip nervously as she ran a hand through her bleached blonde hair. It was cropped close to her scalp on one side and hung long on the other side. Her bright red lipstick and piercing-blue eyes were stark against her pale, anaemic-looking complexion. She was a thin woman, with a narrow face and a sharp beak of a nose.

Scott looked around the cluttered lounge. The sofas clashed with the green carpet. The DVD cases either side of the decorative fireplace overflowed with DVDs. Potted plants lined the windowsill, blocking out some of the natural light, which darkened the room.

"What's happened to Linda?" Jackie searched their eyes for answers.

"Do you know Linda well?" Scott asked.

Jackie shrugged. "Well enough. She is my neighbour and my friend. She doesn't dump Shannon and Leo with just anyone."

Scott produced a small evidence bag containing Linda Allen's driving licence. "Is this the person who lives across the road? Who you know as Linda Allen?"

Jackie's eyes narrowed as she focused on the small pink card. She nodded once in confirmation.

"And when was the last time you saw her?"

"Sunday," Jackie replied, a hint of frustration in her tone.

"What time would that have been?"

She sighed. "Afternoon, I guess. I did her hair for her, and then she dropped off the kids before heading out for a date. Look, are you going to tell me what is going on?"

Helen, who had been making notes up until now, took over the conversation. Her voice was softer and more sympathetic. "We've discovered the body of a woman, and we believe it might be Linda Allen. A handbag was found nearby, and this driving licence was in the purse. We can't be certain it's Linda for sure, but we suspect it to be the case."

A mixture of surprise and fear appeared to overwhelm Jackie. Her face fell faster than a corpse in cement boots. In that instant her skin greyed, her mouth parted slightly, and her eyes widened.

Helen sat beside her. She held Jackie's trembling hand.

"What happened to her?" Jackie asked.

"We are unsure at the moment," Helen said. "She was discovered this morning."

Jackie gasped in shock, her eyes misting at the thought of her friend. A cascade of guilt flowed through her as she remembered cursing Linda.

"Can you tell us any more about the date?" Helen asked softly.

"She didn't really say anything. She said she'd met him online and was looking forward to a fun night. She didn't mention his name, and I didn't ask."

"Had she met him before?"

Jackie shook her head. "No, I don't think so. She wanted to make a great first impression. So, I did her hair for her."

"Do you know the website she used? Or where she was meeting him?"

Jackie didn't answer, just stared at the floor.

After a moment she said, "What about her kids?" She flicked her head in the direction of the kitchen.

"We'll contact social services and they'll take care of them. They start by contacting the next of kin."

Jackie offered the smallest of sarcastic laughs. "Good luck with that. I don't think she and her mum get on too well...How did she die?"

Scott and Helen exchanged the briefest of glances.

"I'm afraid I can't discuss the details of the case. It's an ongoing investigation, but we suspect foul play," Scott said.

"Murdered...?"

"We suspect so."

"I can't believe it. She was so excited about the date. She had even bought red underwear because the fella she was meeting said he was into that."

"Where did she work?" Scott asked.

"She worked for BoxK4, on the Hyde Business Park. She handled phone calls for them. Customer agent or something. I can't remember the exact title."

"Had she been seeing anyone from work?"

"I don't think so. But she did get on very well with the guy she'd met online. They seemed to connect, almost in a familiar kind of way."

"As if they knew each other already?" Scott probed.

"I'm not sure about that. But they seemed to share similar interests, and it was as if he knew what she was thinking before she even said it sometimes. If she had been the suspicious type, she would have thought someone was stalking her because he knew her so well."

Scott could relate to that. His previous case involved a suspect who had stalked him. And it had felt like an invasion of privacy, which left an uneasy feeling.

"She only wanted fun," Jackie said. "Linda wanted some company and excitement in her life. Between working and juggling two young kids, she deserved a break. But this...Did she suffer?"

"No," Scott lied. "She didn't give you a name? Tell you what he looked like? Or the car he drove or where he worked? Anything at all about him?"

"No. No. I told you, she said fuck all. She didn't tell me, and I didn't ask. Yeah, I'm a nosey cow. But she'd been on a few dates before him. And I gave up asking."

"She had been in previous relationships? " Scott asked. "Can you tell me about them?"

"There's not much to tell. She'd had a few online dates, but nothing came of them. They were more like one-night stands, if you know what I mean. She enjoyed her sex. So, I guess it suited her well. She was knocking about with a married fella at one point, but she never told me who it was."

"Anyone else?"

"Then she had another boyfriend, but he was a tosser. She was married once, but he was a bit handy with his fists, if you know what I mean." Her eyes flitted between Scott and Helen, who both nodded their understanding.

"This led to her going online?" Scott asked.

"Yeah. And she got loads of replies. I got the impression there were more men on these sites than women. She was bombarded with replies. Some right weirdos who sent pictures of their cocks. She was upfront about it and told blokes that she had kids. That weeded out some of the replies but a few stuck around."

"After she left on Sunday, you didn't hear from her again?"

"No. I kept looking out of the window hoping I'd see her car back on the drive. I tried her phone dozens of times, but it went to voicemail. I was getting frantic. I thought I was only looking after the kids for an evening."

Helen leant in. "I know this is a difficult thing to ask of you, but we need someone who knew her to identify the body. The sooner we can do that the sooner we can confirm that it is Linda."

Jackie shuddered. "Jesus fucking Christ, do I have to?"

"You don't have to. But it would help our investigation, and someone needs to do it. It won't take long, and one of us will be with you all the time."

Jackie nodded, even though uncertainty reflected in her body language as she wrapped her arms around her.

Scott stood and walked over to the window, where he stared out at the quiet street. "We also need to identify her next of kin."

"Well, I guess you could say it was her mother, but good luck in getting through to her. They don't see eye to eye."

He turned to face her. "Who else?"

"You've got John Richards. That's her ex. He's Shannon's dad. He's the one handy with his fists."

"And the reason she left?" Scott asked.

Jackie didn't answer. "Then she was with Andrei Dalca, her boyfriend."

"Father of the baby?"

Jackie shook her head, confusion etched on her brow. "Not as far as I know. But to be honest it got complicated after that. I think she was having an affair with a married man, and little Leo was the outcome. Dalca found out about it and kicked the relationship into touch."

"Who was the married man?"

Jackie shrugged one shoulder. "Your guess is as good as mine, unless you're Mystic Meg."

"Where can we find Dalca and Richards?" Scott asked.

"Dalca works at that big DIY warehouse on the Hollingbury retail estate. I'm not sure where he lives. He seems to move about. Richards on the other hand, the fucking drunken bastard, he'll be anywhere he can sit in peace and drink beer all day long. So good luck on finding him. Personally, I think he lays low, so he doesn't have to pay child support for Shannon."

Scott made a few notes in his notepad before asking a

final few questions. "And what's the situation with her mum?"

"Linda's dad was a drunk who just fucked off. He was told he had cirrhosis of the liver one day, disappeared the next. Linda and her mum got on okay until little Leo came along. Her mum just flipped when she found out about Linda having an affair with a married man. Something wasn't quite right there."

10

Scott and Helen waited around for another hour after visiting Jackie Cartwright. With the recent discovery of the purse and a set of keys, Scott was confident the latter would allow them access to Linda Allen's house. Matt's team had completed a forensic analysis of the keys and sent them over with a constable.

He opened the door and he and Helen stepped inside.

Jackie's house was cluttered, but Linda's was worse. Toys and board games were stacked up in one corner of the lounge. The room was in dire need of a lick of paint. Floorboard peeked through holes in the threadbare carpet. The sofa cushions were sunken, imprinted with the shape of several rear ends. Several empty bottles of wine and just as many glasses sat gathered on the small table to one side of the sofa. Scott wondered if Linda had been drinking alone or with company. Forensics would confirm that.

A distinct and unpleasant odour lingered in the air. Damn disgusting...toddler nappies. He scrunched his nose and continued looking around.

An Xbox and several controllers lay strewn on the floor close to the TV. Washed baby clothes covered every square inch of space on two clothes horses beneath one window. From the damp smell, it was evident the room hadn't been aired in many days.

The messy theme continued through to the kitchen. Dirty plates filled the sink, open cereal packets collected on the table where they had last been used, and rubbish overflowed from the kitchen bin.

Scott went from room to room, finding no evidence that Linda had fought off an attacker. The general untidiness resulted from a lack of care and attention rather than violence.

Upstairs was no different to the ground floor. The children's bedrooms had clothes thrown on the floor; toys had been discarded where they were last used; their beds were unmade. One thing that caught Scott's attention was the difference in quality of the items in Leo's room compared to Shannon's. Shannon's bedding appeared to be cheap and gaudy, her furniture tatty, and her clothes from the cheap and cheerful Primark. Leo's room puzzled him. The room had new furniture including a strong and robust cot, and judging by the few labels that he had checked, the items of clothing had been bought from John Lewis.

Linda's room resembled an adult version of Shannon's. An ironing board set up in a corner had a basket of washing underneath, ready to be ironed. It also served as a temporary resting spot for a large bag of makeup, the contents strewn across its surface. Several outfits were laid out on the bed as if waiting to be tried on. Scott assumed Linda had been considering which outfit to wear on Sunday evening. Various items of underwear lay scattered across a bed, several still with shop tags on.

An empty shoebox piqued Scott's attention. The box label identified its contents as a pair of black-patent, peep-toe heeled shoes, with ankle strap fastenings and a slim stiletto heel. Scott searched around on the floor and in the wardrobes looking for shoes that matched the label, but decided that she must've worn them for her date. That her body had been discovered without the shoes ramped up his curiosity.

Helen inspected the small chest of drawers by Linda's bed and found a pink vibrator, condoms and a pair of handcuffs. As she continued her search, the second drawer revealed several photocopied images of Linda in various stages of undress and posing provocatively.

Scott and Helen pulled out of the house when the SOCOs arrived.

"You're trying to embarrass me, aren't you?" Scott teased, upon return to the office.

Abby spun in her seat and smiled warmly at him. She stood and gave him a friendly hug.

"It looks like you caught the sun," he remarked. "Judging by your tan, you had some decent winter sunshine."

"Yes, it was decent most days. There was the odd cloudy day, but we had sunshine and temperatures into the late teens and early twenties. You didn't tell me that El Faro had its own little microclimate. Sharon and Sean told me that the weather was like that nearly all year round."

Abby followed Scott to his office and filled him in on the

holiday while he unpacked his briefcase and fired up his computer.

He was desperate to ask the one question that had weighed heavily on his mind since Abby had left but held back. He'd just seen her.

"Did the kids have a good time?" he asked instead.

Abby grinned from ear-to-ear – a smile that Scott had not seen for some time. It was gushing and bathed in happiness and contentment. Her smile took away all the worry lines and creases that often left her looking embattled, weary and older than her years. She nodded enthusiastically and rolled her eyes.

"They loved it. It's such a laid-back lifestyle over there. No one's in a hurry to do anything. We went out to eat a few evenings, and as typical Brits, we went out at seven p.m. and the restaurants were empty. We would leave at nine p.m. as the Spaniards were just arriving. The kids loved the whale-shaped pool on the complex. They were in and out constantly; the cold didn't seem to bother them. I've never seen them look so happy."

"Truth be told, standing here now, I've never seen *you* look so happy."

A comfortable silence lingered between them as they stared at one another. No words needed to be said as Abby's eyes conveyed a thank you.

They made their way out to the main floor for the team briefing. Abby had caught up with Mike earlier, so she knew the bare bones of the case.

Scott said, "Right, we need to start checking with the NCA. Look for any similar cases over the last two to three years. We should have a positive ID on the victim later today. Helen's accompanying Jackie to the morgue, but from the evidence we've gathered so far, we know we're dealing with the murder of Linda Allen."

"Cara confirmed it was strangulation rather than suffocation?" Abby asked.

"Yes, in her opinion."

"So why the plastic bag taped around her head?"

Scott stuffed his hands in his pockets and did his usual walk around the incident board. "That's something we're not sure of now, Abby. Maybe he wanted to suffocate her and panicked, or maybe it wasn't quick enough for him. It's anyone's guess."

"I've just checked her social media profiles," Mike added. "Nothing jumps out at the moment. Just lots of pictures of her kids, the usual Mummy thing."

Scott nodded. "Whilst you're at it, Mike, can you check her banking records, social security, and look for friends, boyfriends, ex-boyfriends, her ex-husband, family and work colleagues? Jackie Cartwright, her neighbour, said she worked at BoxK4. Can you find out a bit more about them, and who owns it?"

Mike offered an affirmative nod. "I'll check PNC, to see if she's had any run-ins or bother."

Scott perched on the edge of one desk, several ideas racing through his mind. "Whilst you're checking banking records, Mike, can you see if any payments went out for anything that might resemble a dating service? Jackie said Linda had put her profile on a dating website and had met people through it. Most of these sites leave a breadcrumb trail. Let's see if we can narrow down where she may have met her date."

Helen jumped in. "Guv, the search teams are still scouring the area. They believe they've discovered her phone. It matches the description that Jackie gave us. A Samsung S5 Gold. It's with forensics. They will download its contents for us."

Scott thanked Helen for the update. The discovery of Linda's phone was one thing that Scott could cross off his mental checklist. Its absence had bothered him ever since her handbag had been found. His early hypothesis was that it had either been dropped or discarded.

Abby crunched over the facts as she absorbed the different details being thrown about.

"Guv, she was dressed up to go out," she said. "Jackie said that Linda had bought a new top, a silver skirt, fresh underwear and new shoes. I just wonder if she was set up and invited out?"

"To be raped and then murdered?"

Abby shrugged. "It's plausible. She was found partially dressed. But her knickers, skirt and shoes are missing. She must have been driven up there, or driven herself there because of its remoteness, so either those items are in her car, the car of the perpetrator, or they were kept as souvenirs?"

It was a fair point, and one he had already considered. The missing items needed to be found. He would go to Meadows, begging bowl in hand, and ask for extra resources. If those items were discovered, valuable forensic evidence would help to progress the case. The silver duct tape used to secure the bag over her head was already undergoing extensive forensic analysis with a company that Matt used in Cambridge.

Matt had informed Scott that duct tape had three constituents: a polymeric backing, an adhesive, and fabric reinforcement, or scrim, between the backing and adhesive.

Extensive analysis would be conducted on the composition and physical construction of the sample. Matt went on to say that scientists would then examine the tape sample for different traces such as finger marks and human biological deposits.

The team considered a few more options before a call came through to confirm that uniformed officers had located a Vauxhall Corsa, its index number confirmed that the vehicle belonged to Linda Allen. The car had been discovered in The Greys Pub car park in Southover Street. Scott had asked the officers to seal off the area until he arrived and requested scientific services to attend the scene.

11

Southover Street boasted a narrow road with a long, steep incline. Close to the university and with easy access into town, it was a popular rental spot with students looking for cheap, multi-occupancy accommodation. It was also a street where you needed a healthy set of lungs and a strong resolve to make it to the top.

The Greys Pub didn't resemble much of a pub from the outside. Painted a garish green and with brown framed windows, it looked more like a house. But its grungy appearance suited the social demographics of those who went there. Mainly students, with the odd spattering of locals, were attracted by its intimacy and cheap prices. Those passing or new to the area wouldn't even know of its existence.

Scott and Abby pulled up alongside a police squad car. To one side of the pub were a small cul-de-sac and car park that the pub shared with nearby residents. The presence of police had attracted the odd, curious passer-by but in the main, students gave no more than a cursory glance before continuing their journeys.

"How does it feel to be back on the job?" Scott asked Abby, as he stretched his shoulders and glanced around to take in his surroundings.

Abby smiled. "Ask me at the end of the shift."

It felt good to have Abby back. He had taken for granted the little things they used to do, like going to Munch for a quick break, or getting something to eat after a post-mortem.

"Not the best location for a first date, is it?" Scott said.

"Well, put it this way, if someone took me for a date here, it would be the first and last one."

Scott agreed with her assessment. It appeared to be an unusual setting. He imagined most people would pick a place in the centre of town, somewhere in The Lanes, with a bright cosy atmosphere and high visibility for security.

The dusty, battered Corsa sat in one corner of the car park. Enquiries confirmed that the vehicle had been there since Sunday evening.

Scott ducked under the tape surrounding the car and peered in through its dirty windows. Empty drink cartons and crisp packets filled the footwells; a spare jumper sat on the back seat; a smart, expensive car seat was strapped into the rear. There were no signs of a struggle or anything to suggest that something untoward had happened inside the vehicle.

After the vehicle had been examined at the scene, Scott would arrange for its removal for further analysis. SOCOs would look for any biological traces like blood, semen, and hair, and clothing fibres they could use as part of the elimination process.

He and Abby entered the pub next.

Its interior was dark and far smaller than Scott had expected. The low ceiling added to the claustrophobic atmosphere. Abby scrunched up her nose and pulled her arms tighter to her sides, as if imaginary germs might leap out from the seat cushions and walls. A few people propped up the bar, supping casually on their pints. The police activity added excitement to what was likely a quiet and boring visit to the pub. The walls were covered in an assortment of posters and pictures. At the far end was a small stage area, where local bands likely played most evenings.

A man with a bushy grey beard and rotund belly introduced himself as Jeff, the landlord.

"What's going on outside?" Jeff asked.

"We're investigating a serious incident involving the driver of a vehicle in the car park. A green Vauxhall Corsa." Scott held up a picture of Linda Allen that he had taken from her house. "We're wondering if this lady was in the pub on Sunday evening? She's the owner of the vehicle."

Jeff scratched his eyelids as he leant over the counter to examine the picture. The edges of his mouth turned down as he shook his head. "I can't say I remember her. As you can see, we're a small pub, and at the weekends it's standing room only. I don't remember her, but that's not to say she wasn't here."

"Were you serving all evening on Sunday?"

Jeff nodded. "Pretty much, apart from taking a few breaks to go for a piss."

"Was anyone else serving?"

"Only Amber. She works a few days a week. A student at the uni. Amber was here on Sunday night. Let me give her a shout. She's downstairs sorting out the crates."

Scott nodded. "That would be helpful. This lady would

have been wearing a white top, a short silver skirt, and black stilettos. She may have turned a few heads dressed like that, had she come in here."

Jeff tugged on his beard. "Maybe so, but she doesn't ring a bell."

A few minutes later, a short, thin girl appeared who barely looked in her teens. A ponytail of dark brown hair swayed behind her as she wiped her hands. "Can I help? Jeff said you wanted to see me."

Scott and Abby introduced themselves and explained the reason for their visit. "Did you see this lady on Sunday night?"

Amber took the photo and studied it intensely. "I'm not sure. The face looks a little familiar."

"She was wearing a white long-sleeved top, a bright silver skirt, and black stilettos."

Amber thought for a few moments until her memories caught up. "Yes, I remember her. She wasn't in here for long. Maybe ten or fifteen minutes. She sat alone by the door, kept glancing at her phone, and then looking around the pub. We tend to get people in here who dress more *casually*. She looked as if she was ready to go clubbing."

"And how did she come across to you? Did she look relaxed, or nervous?"

"Nervous as fuck. One minute she was checking her phone, the next minute she was checking her appearance in her phone, and then playing with her hair, and then looking around again. That's all she did."

"And did anyone turn up?" Scott asked.

Amber hesitated for a moment. "I'm not sure to be honest. I saw her grab her phone at one point and answer it.

And whilst she was on the phone, she looked out of the window. Almost as if the person calling her was outside?"

The girl paused for another moment as she scratched her head and recalled the night. "I don't know. Maybe I imagined it, but I remember her stepping outside and looking at the shadow of a man. Whether that was the person she was waiting for, or whether it was one of our customers having a cheeky fag outside, I don't know."

"Was there anything you noticed about the person outside?" Abby asked. "Were they white, black, tall, short – what they were wearing? Anything like that."

Amber shook her head as her brow furrowed. "Nope. Think he was white. It was too dark, and we were too fucking busy for me to take notice. Why, what's happened?"

Scott reassured her she had been more than helpful and said nothing other than they were investigating a serious incident.

After thanking the barmaid and Jeff, they made their way outside and scanned the street. Scott asked Abby to get a few uniformed officers over to the pub in the evening to interview the regulars. "Smokers need somewhere to go; I wouldn't be surprised if there were a few customers outside at the time Linda left."

Abby stood on the corner of the street and peered down the road towards town. "There was no CCTV in there and nothing out here, either. I assume that person who called her phone was the person she had a date with, but it doesn't feel right. Look at this place, guv," she said, gesturing to the building. "It's a tiny little grungy pub. Hardly a place you'd want to go for a first date, or even meet at before going somewhere else."

Scott didn't have the answer. The date could have been

legitimate, if not a little unorthodox, and perhaps someone else had killed her later that night. But that didn't explain why her car was still here. In fact, there were a lot of questions that Scott couldn't find answers for.

"How about we grab lunch? We can talk about sex."

Abby spun round and stared in confusion. "Scott, you're a great boss, and I love you as a friend, but I think you're pushing your luck. I'm spoken for, remember?"

Scott rolled his eyes. "You should be so lucky. I like my women with more meat. As for you, I've seen more meat on a chicken satay."

Abby punched his arm in protest. "You men are all the same.

They headed back to the car. 'So, what did you mean by sex, then?"

"Perhaps this was nothing more than a sex game gone wrong and the guy panicked. But what if he's done this before and we're missing the connection?"

12

The morgue hallway had as much personality as the rest of the building, with slate-grey floors and dove-coloured walls. Polystyrene squares laid out in a grid-like pattern covered the ceiling. The commercial prints on the wall were tasteful in the dullest kind of way.

"You look a bit peaky. Are you okay?" Helen asked.

Jackie stopped biting her bottom lip. She could hear her pulse banging in her ears; sweat dripped down her back. She tried to return the smile, but her lips barely twitched. She curled her fingers around the strap of her handbag and tried to control her rapid breathing.

"I've not seen a dead body before, and it's even worse because it's my friend. This whole place gives me the creeps. I don't know if I can do this. What happens if I pass out? What happens if I chuck up?" Her jaws chattered, as fear gripped and panic laced her tone.

Helen offered her a sympathetic smile and rubbed her arm. "She will look very peaceful, as if she is asleep. The covering will come up to just beneath her chin so all you will see is her face. We don't need to hang around; it will literally take just a few seconds. I just need you to have a look at her, so that we can be absolutely sure that it's Linda Allen."

Neil, the mortuary technician, broke the tension by opening the door and waving them through to the visitors' room. Several chairs hugged the perimeter, and a small table sat to one side. A small crib sat atop. The sight of it took Jackie's breath away. She assumed this was where dead babies were placed prior to identification. There was a softer feel to this room, which was in marked contrast to the hallway. A large, glass plate window overlooked a secondary sterile room with a hospital gurney and the silhouette of a body beneath a white shroud.

Jackie's eyes were transfixed by the ghostly image. Helen took her by the arm and gently coaxed her towards a plate glass window. Neil stood on the other side, standing by the cadaver. Jackie gave Helen a nod, who in turn nodded at Neil. He lowered the shroud.

Jackie stared at the ashen face of her friend. Helen had been right; Linda looked asleep, just as Helen had described. "Yes...that's Linda." She sniffed and wiped a tear away with the back of her hand.

Farther down the corridor was a small, but comfortable relatives' room. It contained a few comfy chairs, a small table with a box of tissues and a lamp on it. Helen had arranged for two cups of tea. She led Jackie Cartwright to one seat.

"Are you okay?" Helen asked.

Jackie nodded softly as she stared at the steaming cup. "Linda had a rough life. All she wanted was to be happy. In fact, all she dreamt about was a new life. That's why she tried most of the normal dating websites, but never had much luck. She had the odd date here and there, but as soon as she said she had kids, it seemed to sour the atmosphere. She never saw the men again."

"Did any of them work out?"

"She said she had met a decent guy, but he was married. Isn't that always the case? The good ones are always married, and the biggest shits."

"Did she say much about the married man?"

Jackie shook her head. "I did ask, but she kept details about that one close to her chest. I dunno. I think she had a soft spot for him."

"What sort of person was she?" Helen probed.

"Just like anyone else. Happy-go-lucky, liked a bit of fun, and tried her best to be a good mum, but there was a part of her that just wanted so much more from life. She was a bit selfish in that respect, insofar as I guess she longed to feel wanted, and she slept around a bit to get that."

"What about her husband?"

"John Richards," Jackie explained. "A complete tosser. He didn't have a caring bone in his body. He was only interested in himself, his drink, and the bookies."

Helen nodded. "And Dalca, the boyfriend?"

Jackie's face twisted in disgust. "He wasn't much better. Neither of them treated her with the respect she deserved. But this married fellow seem to float her boat. Typical, hey?"

"What happened there?"

Jackie didn't answer, lost in thought, as she continued. "Linda just wanted a bit of fun and sparkle in her life. She did her job, came home and looked after kids. Her life was always about everyone else. Her employers, her kids. It was never about her. All she wanted was someone to care for her. I guess in the end she just wanted to feel loved. Her sleeping around and jumping on these weird dating sites was her way of doing that."

Helen could sympathise. It was a basic human desire to feel wanted and loved. In her line of work, she had seen many examples of where that desire had become distorted, leading to crimes of passion.

"What can you tell me about Richards? I remember you saying that he was Shannon's father."

Jackie frowned. "Richards was a nasty piece of work. He came home one night and found her in bed with another fella. Well, you can imagine what happened."

Helen nodded, but remained silent.

"He hit the roof, and just went mental. He started smashing the place up. Linda got a few cracked ribs, and the other fella just grabbed his stuff and ran out the house naked. The lover didn't get away scot-free; Richards gave him a few slaps. But his real anger was aimed at Linda. I told her to tell you lot, but she was too scared."

"What happened after that? Did they separate?" Helen asked.

Jackie shook her head angrily. "Did they, fuck! He'd get pissed up, then come around banging on the door all hours shouting abuse and threatening to break her legs. He said if he couldn't have her, then nobody else could. As I said, he was a nasty piece of work."

"And she reported this?"

"I don't know, to be honest. I think she feared getting the police involved, because it only seemed to make Richards angrier. They lived separate lives after that. They did their own thing. Got divorced just under three years ago."

"Who came into her life next? The married man?"

Jackie nodded.

"And she continued to see him after she met Dalca?"

"Yep."

"And what was her relationship like with Dalca? Did things get better for her?"

Jackie gave the smallest of laughs. "Not a chance. It seemed to be history repeating itself. He didn't kick her around or anything like that; it's just that they didn't get on. I guess she hoped it would be different this time, but he would much rather sit in the dark and look at porn on his computer into the early hours of the morning than get in bed with her. I just found that really weird."

Helen had a look of surprise on her face; her eyes narrowed. "Why do you say that?"

"Because he liked filthy porn, Linda said. He loved watching all the spanking, the toys, threesomes, that type of stuff. And yet she said she was adventurous and loved all that stuff. The two things didn't make sense to me."

"Is that why they split up?"

Jackie's eyes widened. "No chance. She got up the duff. Immaculate Conception or what? They weren't even having sex that often. So, he told her to fuck off."

"But it could have been Dalca's kid?"

Jackie shrugged. "And don't ask me who the married fella was, because I haven't got a clue. I didn't see him, and she never mentioned him by name. There was no way she was going to spill the beans."

Helen's mind spun with the information. All three men were likely suspects. Two exes and a scorned, married lover.

Jackie proved to be a goldmine of information, as she continued to spew more insight on Linda's life.

"They weren't together for long."

"Linda and the married man?"

Jackie nodded. "Yeah. I don't know why. But it wasn't long after Leo came along when they broke up. Linda was pretty upset about it. She kept saying that she felt used, and that he never really loved her."

"It sounds like she had a pretty confusing and tough time in life," remarked Helen.

Jackie agreed. "She didn't want a lot, and she certainly didn't deserve this."

SCOTT WAS BACK at his desk when Helen returned from the mortuary that afternoon. She recited the salient points of her conversation with Jackie. Scott asked her to add them to the incident board as they continued to pool information.

Once again, he relied on his trusted notepad and pen to jot down the key players in this case, and drew tenuous links between them all. He searched through databases and chased up names. Neither Richards nor Dalca were known to them. Jackie's hunch had been right. Linda hadn't involved the police after Richards assaulted her. But the married lover was still an unknown quantity.

After further checks and several hours later, Scott leant back in his chair and cracked his stiff back. Something sat uncomfortably with him. The police databases had thrown up a case that piqued his interest and raised his concerns.

It was a case that matched key characteristics of his current investigation. A rape and murder nine months ago in Cardiff.

Their unknown suspect had done this before.

13

It was late in the evening when Scott briefed Meadows on the findings of his research, as well as given him a general update on how the case was progressing.

Scott noticed that even after a full day's work, Meadows's shirt was still immaculate, as if he'd ironed it several times during the day. Perhaps it was because Meadows hardly left his office, a gripe that annoyed Scott.

Scott had met his fair share of superintendents before, and they'd all had their own unique management style. Some preferred to be amongst the team, supporting them and being involved in their cases. Others, like Meadows, adopted the hands-off approach, preferring to attend meetings, being seen where they needed to be seen, and delegating as much as possible. They rarely put in the long hours. For many, it was a nine-to-five job with weekends off. The perk of the senior ranks.

Scott sighed out his frustration as his team gathered around the incident board.

"How are we getting on with our various lines of enquiry?" He scanned the team.

Mike chipped in first. "I've been checking her social media profiles. So far, I've looked at Facebook and Instagram. She doesn't have any other social media accounts that I can find. There's nothing on her Instagram account other than pictures of her kids, and various images she's reposted. Facebook is the same. She's got one hundred and seventy-three friends, though I doubt many are real friends. I'll go through the list, but it's a piss-poor, boring job."

Scott agreed, but any male friend needed to be chased up before moving on to the partners of female friends in her list. He doubted many were true friends, but friends of friends, where she'd accepted their friend request out of politeness. Or likely a random connection rather than anything else. He doubted if she'd spoken to many of them.

Helen chimed in next. "Jackie seemed to suggest that Linda didn't have a lot of friends. She was too busy at work or busy running a household as a single parent. They would pop over to each other's houses for a quick cuppa, but other than a date here or there, Jackie suggested Linda didn't have much of a social life."

If Helen's assessment was correct, then most of the Facebook friends were nothing more than virtual friends.

Helen finished her update on her conversation with Jackie at the mortuary.

Scott said, "Mike, I know you are waiting for some feedback from NCA, so I chased them on your behalf. They seemed slow to pull their finger out. In combination with their feedback and my research, I've narrowed it down to one unsolved stranger rape case from nine months ago. It happened in Cardiff. A twenty-nine-year-old female called

Daisy Callaghan. It appears to carry the same MO. The victim contacted her assailant through an online dating site, and someone picked her up from a pub."

"Definitely an online dating site?" Helen asked.

"Without a doubt. Having read the case file, it's too similar for us to ignore. You've got a lone female sitting in a pub just by the door. In fact, she had been told to sit by the door. She was kept waiting. Just in the same way that Linda had. Amber the barmaid at The Greys Pub recalled Linda sitting by the door."

The revelation piqued everyone's interest.

"Any description, guv?" Abby asked.

Scott shook his head. "Not much other than he was white and wearing a hoodie. Yet he came into the doorway of the pub, exchanged a few words with the victim, and left with her."

"Are we assuming that our assailant is an IC1?" Abby asked.

"Well, it's a starting point, unless we have other evidence to contradict it."

Scott pinned a picture of Daisy Callaghan to the notice board. She had light brown hair, a warm smile, and full cheeks. She was a single parent to one young boy aged seven.

"They found her on Roath recreation ground. The same pattern of injuries. Compression to the neck, and a Tesco carrier bag over her head. The only difference was that the carrier bag wasn't taped tight around her throat, so I assume he didn't have enough time to do that, or simply held the bag in place."

"Is the tape an addition in our case?" Abby asked.

"It's not unheard of for a killer to become more sophisticated in their killings. They often refine their techniques as they become bolder and their confidence grows."

"What now, guv?" Abby asked.

Scott stared at the incident board, and the pictures of two innocent women stared back at him. Both had been seeking excitement in their lives, both had been struggling with the responsibilities of single parenthood.

"Based on Helen's information, I think a good place for us to start is with her previous relationships. We need to investigate Richards and Dalca. We haven't got information on her married lover, so we need to park him to one side until further information comes to light." Scott got closer to the photos. "She didn't have a computer, so everything must have been done through her phone. The high-tech unit should have that information by tomorrow. Thankfully, her phone wasn't password protected. We should get access to her gallery of photographs, messages in Facebook Messenger, and emails. I'm hoping we'll find out which dating app or site she was using."

Linda and Daisy were victims of a growing trend. The NCA had provided Scott with recent evidence to suggest a four hundred and fifty percent rise over the past five years in stranger rapes involving online dating apps. With the fact that one in three relationships often began online, and with seven million UK users registered with online dating sites, that figure was set to rise.

The NCA had gone on to add that with online dating, including free and subscription services, dating websites, apps and 'hook-up' services, early analysis indicated that the online dating phenomenon had produced a new type of sexual offender. These offenders were less likely to have criminal convictions, but instead were exploiting the ease of access and armchair approach to dating websites. The overall danger was often aided by potential victims not treating their potential matches as strangers. In a virtual world, it was too easy for vulnerable women to entertain the idea that an intimate connection already existed between them and a stranger. The research suggested that victims felt comfortable meeting their dates as they felt they already knew them.

Scott said, "I plan to contact the SIO for the Cardiff case to see if they can assist us. For all intents and purposes, Daisy had a busy love life, much in the same way that Linda did. They started off with several suspects but could not get a breakthrough."

"Why do you think he targeted Linda?" Helen asked.

Scott pondered her question. He wasn't sure. "Perhaps because she was vulnerable. A single parent desperate for love. If he's connected to the Cardiff case, then he's a serial predator."

"And Linda and Daisy could just be the tip of the iceberg," Abby added.

The thought hung in the air as the team contemplated whether there were other victims yet to be discovered. Their bodies dumped and buried in isolated spots in the hopes they would never be discovered.

Scott said, "We also need to test the DNA recovered from Linda against samples retrieved from Daisy."

"What are your thoughts on the mindset of the killer?" Abby asked, intrigued.

"I think he targets vulnerable women. Women who are lonely, single, and who have a tough life. These women are looking for a way out, and are hoping to meet the man of their dreams, and he's using that to his advantage. Maybe he has a grudge against women. And that either stems from childhood where he wasn't loved by his mother or his past relationships didn't go the way he'd hoped. And this is his way of getting revenge."

"Like a control thing?"

Scott nodded. "Control and payback. And that's why if the Cardiff case is connected to us, then he has become sophisticated in the way he carries out his crimes. He's got braver and more aggressive. It could be the control thing is going to his head. And the level of satisfaction he got from the previous crime doesn't stimulate him as much, so he makes his killing more intense to get the same buzz."

"If that's the case, then the next time he kills, the level of violence could be worse?"

There was a consensus of nods.

"I'm still liaising with the search teams," Mike offered. "They've not located her skirt, underwear or shoes. How long do you want them to continue searching?"

"We'll push for another twenty-four hours. I'm not sure Meadows will allow the additional resources for much longer than that. The items have to be out there, unless he's kept them as souvenirs."

"This married man bothers me, guv," Helen said. "What if Linda wanted more from him and he refused to leave his wife? After all, she wanted a happy-ever-after ending. Maybe she backed him into a corner by threatening to tell his wife? That's a good enough motive."

"I would tend to agree with you, but if it turns out that the Cardiff case was carried out by our attacker, then your theory doesn't fit."

He pulled back the heavy, metal grate that covered the drainage shaft. The coldness of the metal numbed his fingers. In the dark of night his senses remained on high alert, as he listened out for the slightest of sounds and watched for movement in the shadows.

He lowered the metal ladder attached to the shaft wall and descended to the platform below.

She cowered to one side, cold and scared. Her back was pressed against the cold wall, a thin sleeping bag covering her shivering body.

He loosened the cable around her neck, giving her the opportunity to move her stiff limbs. The whites of her eyes penetrated the darkness, staring up at her captor. She flinched each time he touched her, his hands moving in circles as he caressed her breasts. His smile pierced the darkness, his white teeth outlining the surge of excitement he felt. His hand dropped between her legs. Her whole body stiffened once again as terror surged through her veins. She let out a whimpering cry as he caressed her mound, enjoying the satisfaction of inserting his fingers inside her. His breathing was hard and laboured as his cock twitched. It wasn't her time yet.

In a soft broken tone, she pleaded for her life. "Please, please let me go. Please don't hurt me. I want to go home."

Her begging went unanswered; he wiped her down with a dirty towel. The overpowering smell choked him as he tipped a bucket of piss and shit over the edge of the ledge. It made a sloshing sound as it hit the bottom. Rats scattered in different directions before returning to feast.

He changed the butane gas canister in the small, green camping gas heater that he'd left for her. Its warmth offered her the only comfort in her cold, dark and damp prison.

He tore off small portions of a cheese sandwich he had prepared at home and fed her by hand. She reluctantly turned away as each morsel was offered to her lips. A few slaps around her head brought conformity. She cried. Salty tears streaked her face. Snotty trails hung off her top lip. Her hair was knotted, dirty and tangled. He wiped damp strands of hair from her face before gripping her face with one hand, forcing her mouth apart.

"It's either my cock in your mouth or the sandwich. Your choice, you stupid bitch."

Her cries didn't even come close to touching his heart. He imagined the look on her face when it finally happened. Her eyes bulging with pressure, as his powerful fingers pressed deep into her throat, her soft white flesh offering little resistance to his power. That's what it was.

Power.

But it's not her time yet.

He secured the cable around her neck to the bottom of the stairs and began his climb. When he reached the top, he pulled the ladder up and secured it against the wall, returning the tension to the wire.

The metallic screeching of the grate heralded her continuing entombment, her cries and screams drifting away as he disappeared into the darkness.

14

Winter sunshine replaced the greyness of the past few days. Scott peeked out his window and smiled, knowing the sun would bring out the winter visitors. Brighton flourished in the sunshine regardless of the time of year. As the golden globe cast its warmth, it would lift the mood and atmosphere in town. The darkness of winter sucked the life out of Brighton. With a lack of tourists, it was quiet, moody and dull.

Cara groaned and stirred under the covers behind him. He watched her in silence. She had a grace and softness about her, even as she slept. Her dark locks framed her face. Her naked form was warm and inviting. As much as he wanted to crawl back under the covers, he had work. It was his turn to groan as he crept out of the room.

He sat in the lounge, cradling his hot cup of coffee. Due to the nature of his work, he needed these quiet moments alone. His job brought him into contact with the undesirables of society. Sadness often replaced joy and anger replaced calmness, and was accompanied by an ever-present need for justification for all his actions.

His thoughts turned to Claire Allen, Linda's mother. He was still to meet her; meeting relatives of the deceased was never something he looked forward to. That Linda and her mother hadn't been on the best of terms made the situation complex. Death was something he'd experienced on a personal level. Whether relatives believed his sincerity or not, his intentions were always genuine.

The case had many loose ends and a complex web of main characters. Anger, jealousy, revenge, and betrayal were all plausible motives for any of the men in her life to want Linda dead. But another thought tugged on Scott's mind.

What if it's none of them and it's a premeditated attack? Without witnesses or forensic evidence, the case would be dead in the water.

He had a dead woman with a private, complicated and tangled love life, and few friends. There was more to this case, Scott was sure of that. He wasn't sure he'd get all his answers. Only Linda knew and she could no longer speak for herself. If the case was connected to the Cardiff stranger rape and murder, then they may have a serial killer at large, which could either simplify or complicate this case.

"Where's my coffee?" came a croaky voice from behind.

Scott glanced over his shoulder to see Cara rub her eyes and run a hand through her tangled hair. She padded across the cold wooden floor as she headed towards the kitchen.

"I didn't want to disturb you. I have to get in early," Scott replied.

She huffed as she poured herself a cup and joined him. "You were up early?"

Scott sighed. "Yes. I've got a lot on my mind, and I've got

a team briefing first thing this morning. It will be a mental day."

Cara blew on her coffee to cool it. "Don't forget you're picking me up tonight."

Scott froze; it had slipped his mind altogether.

Cara sized him up. "You haven't forgotten, have you...? You have."

Scott stuttered. "No, no. We need to go to Sainsbury's. Right?"

Cara glared at him. "You have. I can't believe you forgot. We agreed a few days ago to pick up prints tonight to go along the staircase."

Scott nodded, trying to sound convincing as he said, "Of course, of course I hadn't forgotten."

Cara smiled before putting her cup on the side and sitting astride Scott. "You are a naughty man, Scott. And I think I need to punish you." She undid the cord on her dressing gown and revealed her naked body. "Now where shall I start?"

SCOTT HAD HIS TEAM TOGETHER. Raj was back, though decidedly ropey. Scott knew Raj wasn't on form, because as they gathered for the team briefing, something was missing. Food. Team briefings and food went hand in hand when Raj was around.

Mike chipped in first. "Guv, uniform have been back to The Greys Pub a few times to interview the regulars and show pictures of Linda. One of the regulars said Dalca, her ex-boyfriend, was in the pub that night. Only for about half an hour, and then he left about fifteen minutes before Linda arrived. It may just be a coincidence," Mike said, lifting one shoulder. "Equally, Dalca could have returned, and he could be the man she spoke to outside. We've not been able to confirm that."

The revelation opened a new line of enquiry.

Scott said, "Well, he's someone we need to have a chat with as soon as possible."

Helen passed around printouts of the messages retrieved from Linda's phone.

The team studied them in silence. Mike, crass as ever, wolf-whistled and chuckled as he scanned each message.

"As you can see, they're racy," Scott said.

"I think they're more than racy," Abby added.

Linda had exchanged messages with five different men over the past six months. Many had started off pleasant. Strangers making social chat and finding out about each other's backgrounds. But as the conversations matured over time they became explicit, with the exchange of images.

Linda had enjoyed suggestions made by several men about the use of excessive force, choking, and breath control to heighten her orgasm. She in return spoke about how sexy she felt dressed in skimpy underwear and stilettos. One of her messages referred to how she enjoyed being taken in the missionary position whilst she dug the tip of her high heels into a man's calves, to inflict some pain on him.

"I want to do things you never imagined doing," Abby read out.

"This could be a sex game gone wrong?" Raj said.

Scott considered his suggestion. That was within the realms of plausibility.

"She seemed to get more excited at the prospect of experiencing both pleasure and pain," Scott said. "She even said to some guy with the nickname 'Truck Man' that she looked forward to having his hands wrapped around her neck whilst he fucked her."

"These guys are perverts. Why meet strangers like this?" Raj asked.

They considered most options and agreed that the consenting parties on these sites gained thrill and excitement by experimenting with their kinks.

Following her research earlier that morning, Helen elaborated on what she'd discovered. "I did an Internet search for this type of stuff. Revealing, I can tell you. It's called 'edge play' and it's a kink activity that can lead to lasting damage or death if practised by those with little experience. It's a submissive and dom set-up."

"So, it was a sex game but taken too far?" Raj asked.

"Maybe. With physical edge play, techniques can include the fun headline fodder we've all seen before: knives, guns, ultra-violence, branding, asphyxiation, fire play, waterboarding, or anything that can easily kill a person."

"Guns? Knives? What the fuck's this? The wild west?"

Helen cast him a dismissive look, annoyed at being interrupted. "Obviously death and lasting damage are things they want to *avoid at all costs*, but the rush of good-feeling neurochemicals that come from some of the extreme pain and immobility in edge play can be unparalleled, for both participants."

Helen's research left the team dumbstruck and speechless.

"And there's an interesting observation worth considering," she continued. "As a starting point, they can create an edge play scenario where they bypass enough mental safety features to give the submissive the impression that almost anything could happen. They are left feeling like there are aspects to the other person's behaviour or the environment that are truly out of their control, *unpredictable*."

A different impression of Linda formed in Scott's mind. She had enjoyed risky sexual encounters and was up for trying new things. Fuelled by fantasies and an open mind, she had used online dating to satisfy her needs.

"Until we get more information from Cardiff police, we focus on Linda's murder," he said. "This is about looking into her life, and her connections. Judging from these ,"– Scott waved the printouts at the group– "we now know Linda had a very complex life and a healthy, or unhealthy – whichever way you see it – sex life."

Helen continued. "She was on two websites. Wife Banger, and Dip and Lick. You can't see her face clearly. She used a side profile pic with her hair brushed across her face. The other pictures show her in various stages of undress, along with full frontals, but her small tattoo is visible."

A collective murmur of laughter filled the silence.

"How do companies come up with these names?" Raj speculated. "Dip...And...Lick. Really?"

The others smiled and laughed.

Helen said, "Her bank records confirm that she had been paying twenty-seven pounds a month for Wife Banger for a six-month subscription. She had only joined Dip and Lick nineteen days ago, so she was on their free, one-month trial. I'm in the process of contacting the companies to see if we can identify who she was talking to on both sites. But I worked on a case like this in my last job, and one thing these companies pride themselves on is protecting their users' identities. They won't be keen on releasing information."

Scott asked Helen to keep him informed.

"Mike, any more from the search team?" he said.

Mike shook his head. "I'm afraid not, guv. There's no sign of her underwear, skirt or shoes. Whilst we have the extra manpower, they've extended the search area. We don't have time on our side. The super could call off the search at any time."

Scott added, "One last thing, go back over all our missing persons files and see if there are any single mums with young children who went missing and shared similar sexual preferences to Linda."

After the briefing, Scott caught up with Abby at her desk. "Are you up to speed with everything?"

Abby blew out her cheeks. "With the case, yes. But I still have eighteen case file reviews to do. The twenty-eight-day review markers have popped up. What are your thoughts on the case? Do you think it's linked to Cardiff?"

Scott lifted his hands in a shrug. "I think they are. They're too similar not be connected. We should know more once we have the DNA analysis. I'm hoping we hear from forensics within the next few hours."

"Hey, listen. I wondered about the apartment in Spain. Do you think Cara's friend would allow me to rent it off her once or twice a year?"

Scott smiled. "You liked it?"

Abby grinned and rolled her eyes. "Liked it? More like loved it. The kids were so happy, guv. I've not seen them so happy in years."

"That's because they were enjoying quality time with their mum. It didn't matter where you were. You could have been in Bognor and they still would have loved it."

She laughed. "I doubt Bognor would have the same

appeal. I'm being serious. Maybe I need to be saving so that I can treat the kids to a break in the sun every year."

"I think that's a great idea. Cara's friend rents it out all the time, so I can't see that would be a problem. You'd get mates' rates anyway. Besides, it would do you a world of good. You look so much happier and healthier."

Abby scrunched her face. "I was a pasty shit before?"

They both broke into loud, thunderous laughter, much to the consternation of the others.

"Right, get yourself sorted, Abby. We need to see Linda's mum and then track down Richards and Dalca."

15

"How's Jonathon these days?" Scott asked Abby as he queued in traffic. "You don't seem to say much about him. Everything going okay?"

Abby stared out of the passenger window in silence, watching everyday life going on around her. By the look on her face, she was deep in concentration, thinking about something. He could spot that look from a mile away, the way she narrowed her eyes and pursed her lips.

"Yeah, everything is fine. We try to see each other as much as we can. But we don't spend near enough time together to make a proper go, if you know what I mean?"

Scott knew that feeling. He glanced at her. "Well, hopefully that can change. Now that we're adjusting your shift patterns and hours it should give you more flexibility, and more importantly, some of your life back."

Abby didn't reply, offering a simple nod.

Oh, she's in deep, reflective thought.

Scott hoped it was good thoughts rather than bad. He

didn't want to broach the subject about her leaving. He imagined it wouldn't take much to push her to leave. And that was something he couldn't risk.

"What's your take on the married man?" she asked.

"I'm not sure, to be honest. I'm just as much in the dark as you are. He has money because Leo's room has been furnished with no expense spared. Maybe he was helping financially with the kid and they fell out about that?"

"That's a definite possibility. It seems to be a bit of a mess, doesn't it? Two exes, a married lover, and someone she met online. And that person could be anybody. For all we know, he could live out-of-town."

"The problem we've got is that most of her messages were in WhatsApp. Not only is that encrypted end-to-end, but the majority were deleted from her phone. Her email messages only confirmed that she had received a new message from each new person who contacted her. Without her passwords, we have no way of accessing the two online dating apps on her phone."

Claire Allen lived in a small, unassuming terraced house to the west of the city centre. A small paved driveway offered just a few feet of space between the front door and the road. Scott and Abby skirted around the black dustbin, overflowing with black bags. They rang the doorbell. It was swiftly answered by a dark-haired woman with thinly plucked eyebrows, wearing a black top and a loud green jacket. She had thin lips and a pronounced chin, and with high cheekbones, her face looked hard.

Her eyes flitted between the two officers on her doorstep. She didn't give Scott an opportunity to finish introducing himself before she butted in. "Your lot have already been round."

With an acid tone, she showed no signs of grief over losing her daughter. Her words were abrupt and lacked emotion.

"May we come in, Mrs Allen? It's in connection with the death of your daughter."

She nodded over her shoulder to invite them in. "Well, you aren't gonna be here for anything else, are ya?" she asked as she disappeared into the house, leaving Abby to close the door behind her.

Abby rolled her eyes at Scott.

Claire led them into the front lounge which, though small, was clean. The room had a laminate floor that gave it a contemporary feel; the furniture was neutral, blending into the cream-coloured walls.

"Can I get you something to drink?" she offered.

Scott declined but thanked her. "We are sorry for your loss and would like to reassure you that we're doing everything we can to identify what happened to Linda."

"That's a little too late, don't you think? She's gone. What difference is that gonna make to her, me, or to her kids?"

Scott nodded sympathetically. "I appreciate your pain, but a crime has been committed resulting in the loss of life. We have a duty to investigate and find the person or persons responsible."

Claire nodded. She turned away from Scott and stared out of the window. Everyday life carried on just a few feet away from them. "She never was lucky when it came to men.

Linda always picked the wrong ones. She had a bit of get up and go in her. A free spirit, if you know what I mean. And it always got her into trouble."

While Abby made notes, she was drawn to the pictures of Linda and her children on the windowsill. Happier times, with Linda cradling her newborn baby and Shannon tucked in beside her.

"Did she always have difficult relationships?" Scott asked.

"As far back as I can remember, Inspector. Even back at school, her boyfriends were a waste of space. They hung around in gangs, smoking weed and being a general nuisance. Linda found that cool. She loved the attention."

"And what was your relationship like with Linda?" Scott chose to leave out the timeframe, knowing Linda and her mum had spoken little in the past year.

Claire's face soured, as if she'd eaten a lemon. Her shoulders stiffened; she pulled them back, forcing her spine upright. "We haven't been on speaking terms or seen eye to eye for a little while, to be honest. She could be a bit of a bloody hothead." Claire laughed, breaking the sombre mood. "I guess she got that from me."

"What caused the rift between you?"

Claire shrugged avoiding Scott's gaze. "I got fucked off with her love life. She wouldn't listen. She never did. I didn't want her marrying Richards. He was a right shitbag and everyone knew it. I tried to warn her off. He was known around town for being free with his fists but would she listen? Would she fuck!" Claire shook her head. "And no doubt you've already found out he caught her in bed with someone and smashed the fucking place up, including her."

"Who was she in bed with?"

Claire shrugged again. "No idea. Maybe someone she met down the pub or met through work. Who knows?" Her eyes briefly engaged Scott's before she nervously flicked them away.

Scott didn't miss that oddity. She'd hardly maintained eye contact with him since their arrival. It was a classic sign of someone hiding something. The phrase 'eyes are the windows to the soul' flashed through his mind.

Claire filled the brief silence quickly by continuing her story. "Dalca wasn't much better. He was a lazy tosser. He didn't treat her much better. I'll give him his dues; he didn't hit her or nothing, but I think it was a non-starter from the beginning. He was a weirdo to be honest. Linda said he preferred watching hardcore porn than going anywhere near her. And trust me, she tried. She kept telling me how she threw herself at him. He just wasn't interested most of the time. I don't know why. She was a good-looking girl. She said they would have sex once in a blue moon. He even gave me the eye."

"At what point did the two of you fall out?" Scott asked.

Claire shook her head in disgust. "When she knocked about with a married man. I drew the line there. I made it very clear I disapproved. She told me it was none of my business, and that he made her happy. What can I do? She's a grown-up woman, not a fifteen year old."

"Did she ever mention a name to you?"

There it was again, another fleeting glance before Claire's eyes darted away.

"Nope. She wouldn't tell me. We had a few arguments after that, and she got fucked off with me sticking my beak in. Then she had Leo. I told her I wasn't happy about not knowing who the father was. I didn't know if it was Dalca or the married man. We didn't talk after that."

SCOTT leant up against the side of the car and looked up and down the street, as Abby paced on the pavement.

"She's not happy about Leo, or who the father is," Abby said.

"There was something she wasn't telling us."

"How so?"

"Did you not notice how she barely looked at me or you for that matter, throughout most of our visit? She was scared that her face might give something away."

"Like what?" Abby asked.

"I don't know. But this married man has something to do with it. The sooner we track down his identity the better it is for us. If you look at Linda's kids, they have both been brought up differently. Shannon's clothes, her room, and even the way she looks, are in complete contrast to Leo. Shannon gets the rejects and cheap stuff. Leo on the other hand has a beautiful room, an expensive cot, and better clothes. Why would she treat him differently to how she brought up Shannon?"

STANDING behind the curtain and anxiously biting her thumbnail, Claire Allen watched the officers drive away. The last thing she needed was for them to turn around and come back with more questions.

When she was sure they were away, she lifted the mobile

phone in her trembling hand and stared at the blank screen for what felt like minutes. Finally, she flicked through her contacts and pressed the green dial button. She had already rehearsed her words. This needed to be handled delicately. Raising Shannon alone would cost a lot of money, and she knew exactly what she needed. She would not mention that Leo didn't fit into her plans, but she'd worry about that later.

16

It never ceased to surprise Scott how quickly normality returned in the wake of any tragic event. The quiet cul-de-sac where Linda had lived was no different. The postman was doing his rounds; an elderly couple was unloading the weekly shopping. They offered nothing more than a quick, cursory glance as Scott and Abby pulled up outside Jackie Cartwright's home. Small floral bouquets had been laid on Linda Allen's doorstep, a silent tribute from neighbours.

Jackie made tea for them before settling down on a sofa to face the officers. She grasped her mug in both hands like a prized possession, worried she might drop it through her trembling fingers.

"How are you holding up?" Abby asked.

Jackie shook her head and stared at the brown steaming liquid, unable to find the right words. It was as if her mouth wouldn't communicate her thoughts.

"Thank you for taking the time to formally identify her body. I know it couldn't have been easy for you."

"I...I..." She shook her head again. Shock had penetrated her to the core. Jackie was white as chalk. Her eyes and mouth were frozen wide in stunned surprise. Although she looked up at Abby, she appeared not to notice her at all.

"I know it comes as a shock, and it will take time to sink in. If there's anything we can do, you only have to call us," Abby reassured her.

The house was more silent than the last time Scott was here. The children were in the care of social services.

Jackie nodded appreciatively. "I...just can't believe it. Just a few days ago she was here getting her hair done, and the next time I see her, she's looking like a waxwork dummy from Madame Tussauds."

"I want to reassure you we are doing everything we can to find out what happened to her. That's why we need your help," Abby said.

"She didn't deserve this. No woman deserves this. I don't want to know the sick details of what happened to her, and I don't suppose you'll tell me anyway. But it scares the fucking daylights out of me that there's a murderer out there. What happens if he knows where she lived? What happens if he'd stalked her and saw her coming over to my place? Am I in danger?"

Her eyes searched Scott and Abby for an answer, seeking their reassurance, and hoping for their protection, before continuing.

"I'll be honest with you, I'm scared. Every time the door knocks I shit myself. It dawned on me this morning...what if I'm next?" Her voice cracked, straining under the nerves that twisted her bowels, and sent waves of panic through her.

"We are hoping this is just an isolated and random attack."

Jackie didn't let Abby finish her sentence. "Hoping? Hoping?" she fumed, with wide eyes.

"I know it may be concerning for you," Abby reassured her, "but if there's anything that worries you, you only need to call. And that's why we need your help in catching the killer."

Abby was using Jackie's fear and concern to their advantage. A desperate Jackie would be more than willing to tell them things to protect herself and restore normality to her life.

"There is nothing you need to feel bad about," Scott added. "No one could have predicted this outcome, not you, not Linda."

"I know, I know. But she was always moaning about feeling lonely, so I told her to be a bit forward. And if it was love that she was looking for, then she needed to go out and find it. Maybe if I hadn't encouraged her, then whoever she met wouldn't have killed her?"

Scott needed to push harder. Jackie was the closest source of information they had and could provide vital new insights that the team searched for. "We know you spoke at length with DC Helen Swift but we want to clarify a few points. Linda had a decent amount of replies to her profile on two adult contact websites we found. Did she say much about them?"

"She said she'd joined a few sites. It seemed to buoy her. She kept saying she still had it because she had so much interest."

"Do you recall her mentioning anything about the personal ads to anyone else other than you?"

"No, she swore me to secrecy. She said only I knew, and her mate at work, Aluna."

"Did she ever show you any of the replies?"

"Only a few. Most of the ones I saw just had pictures of men's cocks and captions like, 'Fancy getting your lips around this?' How's that for an opening line?"

Scott nodded, rolling his eyes. He often wondered what men hoped to achieve by sending pictures of their genitals to random strangers. "And still nothing springs to mind about the man Richards found in bed with Linda?"

Jackie shook her head. "I can't help you on that front. She kept that one tight to her chest. I can only imagine that she met him at work, or through work, or something like that, because she hardly ever went out. Not that I'm a nosey neighbour or anything like that, but in a cul-de-sac you can see who comes and goes. She hardly had any visitors."

"And her relationship with Richards soured after that point?"

Jackie shrugged. "They went their separate ways."

"Did you ever see him being violent towards her?"

"No, I witnessed nothing myself, but he gave her hell on more than a few occasions. I told her to leave him, but she refused. He was moody, especially after he'd had a few beers. He would give her the odd slap when she got on his nerves. I think his mood changed after he found her in bed with someone. He would always check her phone, kept asking a lot of questions, and was a bully. He said women were all the same and he didn't have a nice thing to say about them...or Linda."

Scott changed tack, still probing. "Was her relationship with Dalca any better?"

Jackie laughed. "I don't think *better*, and *relationship* belong in the same sentence when it comes to Linda's love life. He was a fucking weirdo. Apparently, he was on his laptop till the early hours most nights; I'm surprised he didn't get calluses on his hand, if you know what I mean..."

Scott didn't respond to that. "Do you think he would harm Linda?"

Jackie's eyes widened. "Do you think he did it?"

"We are keeping an open mind in relation to everyone." Scott kept things vague. "He was seen in the vicinity the night Linda disappeared."

"I can't imagine it was him. He's not even in the same league as Richards. A weird pervert, yes, a man who batters women, no."

"Do you think Dalca is Leo's father?"

"No. Linda already told me she didn't think it was him. He just upped and left not long after being told about the pregnancy. I don't blame him. Would you hang around?"

Scott and Abby exchanged a glance.

"How was he so certain he wasn't the father?" Abby questioned. "I believe you mentioned that they didn't have sex that often. But that suggests that they *did* have sex?"

Jackie shrugged.

"And Dalca is in a new relationship?"

"Yeah, Lexi Freeman, a twenty-six-year-old redhead. Slim, petite, almost innocent-looking. Bumps in all the right places. Everything that Linda wasn't."

The name spiked Scott's interest.

Frustrated that they were going around in circles, Abby tried again. "The married man. You must know something about him – a name? What he looked like? Any trivial bits of information that Linda may have divulged?"

Jackie shrugged, a blank, unconvincing look fixed on her face. "Seriously, I don't." She shook her head. "She said he was generous, married, and had cash to splash. Linda told him how she was struggling for money. He helped financially after the baby was born. Linda said he would pop by with a couple hundred pounds every week in cash." Jackie's eyes glistened with jealousy, as if her friend had won the lottery.

"How long did that go on for?"

"I don't know. Maybe a few months, two, perhaps three. Then she was ever so upset, always down and crying. Negative in everything she said. I thought it was postnatal depression or something like that, since you hear about it all the time."

"Did she get any help for it?"

"I don't think it was that. After a while she told me she felt betrayed and used."

17

He felt naughty, like a schoolboy playing with his favourite toy when he had been told not to. The shoe and underwear were the only things he could think about as he caressed them. He inhaled the scent from the knickers; they'd been worn. Probably some tart on a night out who had discarded them after a night of passion.

He recalled a story he'd read online in a dogging forum where a woman had fucked her boyfriend in the car after some heavy petting. Her knickers had been damp from the excitement. Not wishing to go home without them, she had dried them on the hot air vent in the car while her boyfriend drove her home.

He smiled as he caressed the high-heeled shoe and imagined perfectly painted toenails through the peep-toe. He stroked the long, spiky stiletto heel before jabbing the tip into his testicles. Erotic pain shot through him; he hardened in seconds. He had carried a fetish for high-heeled shoes for as long as he could remember. There was something elegant and sexy about a woman in high heels. The way it shaped the leg and how it pronounced the calf muscle. As for showing the arch in the instep of the foot...He failed to describe the overwhelming surge of eroticism that flooded every cell of his being.

Minu had never worn heels; she was firmly ensconced in the flat-shoe brigade. When he had suggested that she dress up in sexy underwear and heels, she had been repulsed by the idea.

"We don't do things like that," had been her scornful reply.

She would kill him if she found out what he was up to. She had hit the roof last time. Their relationship had narrowly survived after his promise never to do it again. She had seen his Internet search history and the X-rated magazines hidden in a lever-arch file in the study. She had seen the bank statements detailing the massage parlours he'd visited, and she had seen his scrunched-up boxer shorts tucked under the pile of washing.

Now, he was in the shed at the back of the garden, satisfying his urges and curiosity. The glow of the light reflected off the highly polished patent surface of the shoe. He only wished that the wearer was here with him. Her legs would be wrapped around his waist pulling him in with each thrust, begging to be satisfied, her breasts rocking with the motion, and her high heels calling to be licked. His mind raced like wild horses galloping through fields; his body tensed as his consciousness flooded with erotic fantasies.

He found any opportunity to escape to the shed. When Minu was at work, or in the bath.

For now, he would leave his prize well hidden. Knowing it was waiting here for him only added to the naughty-boy feelings that coursed through his veins.

THE UNIQUE SMELL OF PLANTS, paint and timber greeted Scott and Abby as they walked into the DIY store. With its metal corrugated walls and high ceilings, along with the bleeping noise of small forklift trucks, a symphony of sounds reverberated around the large space. Oversized trolleys were being pushed in all directions by shoppers and tradesmen alike.

Scott was a strong DIY enthusiast, and often liked nothing more than wandering around these cavernous spaces, admiring tools like screwdrivers, cordless drills and SDS drills in a nerdy kind of way. He was well-versed in the difference between a slotted, Phillips or Pozidriv screwdriver.

His face lit up as they walked through, a reaction not lost on Abby. He had told her en route about the forthcoming DIY projects he was planning for his house now that Cara had moved in.

"You are such a weirdo. Only you could get excited walking in a DIY store," Abby teased. "Next thing, you'll be walking around CID with a tool belt hanging off your waist and calling yourself Bob the Builder." She laughed.

"Your obsession is the gym, mine is DIY," he said proudly.

Abby shook her head in disbelief. "I'd keep that to yourself if you value your street rep."

Having asked, they had been informed that Dalca would be towards the back of the store near the electrical section.

"Andrei Dalca?" Scott asked, producing his warrant card.

The man was in a crouched position, stocking the lower shelves. He looked up, peering at them through dark, heavy eyebrows. He stood and straightened up, wiping his hands on his already grubby orange apron.

"Yes, that is me," he replied in a thick, European accent. He avoided eye contact and looked at the floor.

Dalca was shorter than Scott, at around five-foot seven inches. His jaw was strong and angular with high cheekbones, and a chin that reminded Scott of James Dean. He had a thicket of gelled hair with a side parting.

Scott introduced himself and Abby. "We would like to ask you a few questions in connection to an ongoing investigation."

Dalca shifted his gaze around, clearly embarrassed by the unnecessary attention Scott's visit was generating. Shoppers and store employees cast cursory and inquisitive glances in his direction.

"What is it you want?" he asked in a hushed tone.

"We're investigating the murder of Linda Allen."

Dalca's eyes widened for a moment. "How I can help?" His voice was soft, his words clumsily strung together.

"Could you tell us more about Linda, and your relationship?"

Dalca shrugged his bony shoulders. "There is not much say. We were together for a while. But it didn't work."

"Was it more of a casual relationship, or a loving relationship?" Abby probed.

Dalca considered the question for a few moments. He narrowed his eyes and pursed his lips to suggest he wasn't sure. "Both. I liked her, she liked me."

"You weren't together long?"

Dalca offered a shake of his head.

"Did you talk of starting a family?" Scott asked.

"We spoke about children once or twice."

"So why did it end when she fell pregnant?"

Dalca's eyes shifted again between Abby and Scott, his mouth dry, his senses screaming at him like an animal trapped in a snare. "Because the baby was not mine."

"How can you be so certain?"

"Because she was okay. But in bed, we had different tastes. She is a very dirty woman. She likes a lot of things. So, do I. But different things."

"Are you're telling me that you hardly had sex with Linda?"

"True. Sometimes. But when she doesn't cooperate, I'm not interested."

Cooperate. Scott found that an unusual term.

"Was she not interested because of your preferences or because of you?"

Dalca tapped his temple with his finger. "I'm not stupid. I worked out the dates. It's not mine."

"If it's not yours then who is the father?"

Dalca waved his arm in a large arc. "Take your pick. It could be anyone here. It could be any man on the street. She liked cock a lot, and she needed money. She was a whore. A filthy whore."

"Are you suggesting that she was a prostitute?"

"Maybe, maybe not. You find out. Listen I wore rubber on the few occasions we did. She slept around. I didn't want to catch anything." Dalca's voice turned harsh, aggressive and angry.

"So that annoyed you and you left? Were you angry?"

"Of course."

"Angry enough to hit her?"

Dalca's body stiffened. He waved a finger in front of his face. "No, no, no. I did not kill her. You are finding way to send me back home. If someone beats her up, then it wasn't me. Try her ex-husband. She told me many times he hit her when he had been drinking. Why should I hang around and watch her get bigger with someone else's baby? Do you think I'm fucking stupid?"

Scott smiled. "You tell me, Mr Dalca."

Scott's response riled up Dalca further. He slammed his fist on the shelving; the sound echoed around them, causing others to turn in surprise.

"I did not touch her," he hissed through gritted teeth.

"And you left her to it? You didn't want revenge for making you look like an idiot?"

Dalca's jaw flexed as he clenched his teeth harder.

Scott continued to push. The man's pride was clearly dented. "I think someone in your position would be furious and humiliated to find Linda preferred someone else over you. Maybe she deliberately became pregnant as a way of getting rid of you?"

Dalca struggled for each breath as his chest heaved. "I feel sorry for the fucked-up bitch. Getting pregnant made situation worse."

"Where were you on Sunday evening between six p.m. and midnight?" Scott asked.

"I was around. No idea where." Dalca smiled at Scott. "Probably with my girlfriend Lexi. You can check."

"We have witnesses who believe they saw you in The Greys Pub. Is it somewhere that you go often?"

"I go there sometimes. When Lexi gets on my nerves, I go to the pub."

"Did you see Linda on Sunday evening whilst you were there?"

Dalca shook his head.

"Did you speak with or meet Linda after you parted company?"

"We had no contact since we split. If I was in same pub as her, then it by chance," he replied. Frustration and boredom laced his tone.

Scott said, "Linda was seen talking to a man outside the pub not long before she disappeared. It seems convenient that you were both in the same pub, on the same night that she disappeared. Was that you?"

Dalca rocked with laughter. "Inspector, you are asking me the same questions. Either you not hear me or you trick me."

Scott crossed his arms and held a stare. "You didn't answer my question."

There was an uneasy silence between the three and a tense stand-off.

"Not me. I was no longer interested in her. If someone killed her, then it's her own fault for messing people around."

"And when you left the pub, where did you go?"

"I went home to Lexi. I fucked her. Check if you want. Check her phone. She videoed me fucking her." Dalca sneered with the force of his words.

"Can you think of anyone else who could have harmed her?" Scott asked.

Dalca laughed again. "I guess that list is too long. Try Richards or try the little boy's father. He was married, right? He's just as fucked as she was."

"Do you have a name for the married man?"

"No. And I don't fucking care. Whoever he is, they deserved each other."

Scott assessed the man's body language. His arms were

by his sides; his head was tilted to the left. As the conversation progressed, Dalca increased eye contact. They were all signs that either Dalca wasn't hiding anything or he was a great liar.

"As someone who had a relationship with Linda Allen, you don't appear to be upset that she is dead. Or the fact that two children have been left orphaned."

"I feel sorry for children. Linda could have been nice person, but she was too fucked in head."

18

"Dalca's certainly got possible motive. Revenge for her infidelity," Abby suggested, as she forked chips onto her plate.

Scott nodded his agreement. "Despite trying his hardest, he let his anger slip on more than one occasion."

"We'll need to check his alibi, but I suspect his girlfriend will only confirm that he spent the evening with her, especially if the sex was captured on her phone. That will be time and date stamped, which could give him a rock-solid alibi."

"For the time being we should still keep him in the frame. Linda had an affair with a married man, and for a bloke like him, that's nothing short of humiliation."

The cafe that they were in was hot and steamy. On a cold but breezy day, the locals often extended their lunch break, reluctant to go about their day, instead preferring the warmth and comfort of both the cafe and its hot food.

Scott glanced around and saw the usual mix of tradesmen in their work-stained clothes and steel-toe-capped boots, dunking their toast into runny egg yolks. They were in marked contrast to a few young ladies gossiping and giggling, and one or two elderly people who Scott thought looked lost and alone. He watched as they gingerly picked at their food, their bony and skinny fingers reaching out like skeletal tentacles. Others stared into their cups of tea, deep in thought.

He never tired of watching human behaviour, simple and yet so complex and unique. Just in the space of a few square feet around him, thousands of thoughts were being processed every second, decisions being made, outcomes being explored, and feelings being analysed, unnoticed and unheard.

Abby squirted salad cream onto her plate, then dunked her chips in it. "Do you think she just had a bad taste in men, or do you think she was looking for something that she couldn't find?"

Scott furrowed his brow and narrowed his eyes, seeking further clarification from her.

"What I mean is that she never seemed to have a happy or successful relationship. Richards, Dalca, a married man, and God knows who else. And yet the flipside is she was on these dating websites using pictures that left little to the imagination. She was looking for love but hadn't found it. The question is, was she looking for love in the first place?"

Scott leant back in his chair and thought about it. His gaze drifted around the room, taking in the view of those around him. "It could be either. She was trying to find something that was missing in her life. Whether that was a man or the love and security that being with someone offered her is anyone's guess."

Scott's phone vibrated in his pocket. As he pulled it out, Raj's name popped up on the caller ID.

"What's up, Raj?"

"Guv, I just got the medical records back for Linda Allen. She was being treated for depression and anxiety. She went through a period of postnatal depression after Shannon was born, and more recently after Leo's birth. On both occasions she went through six weeks of CBT."

"What medication was she on?"

"Venlafaxine, seventy-five milligrams. The doctor confirmed that she was still taking it, and SOCO discovered a box in her bedside drawer. The GP also confirmed that Linda had been in to see her just over two weeks ago because she was experiencing problems sleeping, had bouts of restlessness and irritability,"

"Anything else?" Scott asked.

"As a matter of fact, yes, guv. Linda had said to her GP that the meds had improved her mood to begin with, which had improved her relationships and sex life. But then Linda came to her more recently, concerned that the meds weren't working because of increased restlessness, impulsive actions, and suppressed sexual urges. The doctor said that she had sensed concern and desperation in Linda's tone and behaviour."

"What course of action did the doctor take?"

"Linda wanted an increase in her dosage. The doctor refused, instead organising for an appointment to be made with the local mental health unit."

"Okay. Thanks, Raj." He hung up.

"Well?" Abby asked.

Scott explained the key points of what Raj had discovered.

"That seems to tie in what Jackie told Helen, guv. She said Linda was very needy, and was desperate to feel wanted, desired and loved. It sounds like she had a pretty troubled life and the bouts of depression had only worsened her perspective on life."

"And not being satisfied in love only added to her desperate plight."

Scott thought about the perception men had about Linda. Had they seen her as a nice person looking for love? Or a sexually liberated woman keen to explore the boundaries of sexual experiences? Or a woman who was perceived as an easy lay, with no ethical or moral compass?

Had Linda been easily bored? It would explain the number of relationships she'd had. Or was there a part of her that had craved excitement without boundaries?

19

Lunch sat heavy in his stomach as Scott stepped out of the car. His belt felt tighter, and his eyes felt heavy. He stretched his arms and pulled his shoulders back, in a futile attempt to inject life into him. He could have crawled back in the car and taken an afternoon nap, after eating far too much, including half of Abby's chips.

Richards lived in a less than desirable run-down council apartment close to the train station. Like most properties in the area, they had little in the way of front gardens, only small concrete spaces just wide enough to fit a dustbin before you'd step onto the pavement. Grime and dust coated the windowsills and windows, and empty cellophane wrappings collected in the doorway, blown in off the street.

Scott rang the doorbell. After a few minutes, a man in a faded-green T-shirt answered the door. He ran a hand over his stubbly beard as he weighed up the two visitors.

"Yeah?" he said in a croaky voice, his tone uninviting and cold.

Scott and Abby held up their warrant cards.

"John Richards?" Scott said.

Richards offered nothing more than a nod.

Scott put a foot in the door frame to prevent Richards from shutting the door on them, if the thought crossed his mind. "We'd like to ask you a few questions. We are investigating the death of Linda Allen, your ex-wife."

Richards sniggered and stepped to one side, to allow the officers to enter.

Abby flared her nose as the smell hit her. A mixture of stale sweat and a lack of clean air overwhelmed her senses. To the right of the corridor was a small kitchen. Empty microwave meal containers littered the work surfaces, along with empty beer cans. But it was the dog faeces scattered on the kitchen floor that made her want to vomit.

"Oh, Jesus fucking Christ," Abby murmured under her breath. She pushed past the doorway, keen to erase the image from her mind.

A small box room that was being used as a second bedroom was opposite the kitchen. Closed curtains hung loosely from a wooden curtain pole. The room was dark and looked to be nothing more than a dumping ground for clothes, newspapers, and several bicycles. Abby found that ironic, considering Richards appeared to have done no exercise in his life. His T-shirt barely covered his large belly that hung heavily over the waistband of his jogging bottoms. Abby suspected he'd *come by* the bikes.

A threadbare carpet lined the hallway, heavily stained. Abby's mind raced thinking about the disgusting possibilities for the stains.

Richards led them into an untidy and cluttered lounge. He didn't offer them a seat but sat down in an armchair that faced what appeared to be a new television. As she glanced around, Abby noticed several iPhones scattered on the sideboard, as well as an iPad and Beats headphones.

Proceeds from crime? She suspected they were stolen goods, going by her first impressions of the apartment and records that suggested he had no means of income.

Abby stiffened and stepped back towards Scott when she noticed a large, white Staffordshire bull terrier slumped in one corner. Its eyes were darker than a cup of coffee; its mouth drooled saliva, and it growled as it eyed the two visitors.

Richards chortled. "Don't mind Oscar. He wouldn't hurt a fly...Unless he didn't like the look of someone..."

Tension rippled in the air, and an uneasy silence followed. Both Scott and Abby knew from experience as beat officers how volatile situations could become with the presence of dogs. Scott had attended several incidents where dogs like Staffordshire bull terriers and American pit bull terriers had turned on officers. The pit bull had a bite force of over two hundred pounds, and officers were always advised to approach such dogs with caution.

Scott said, "I think for all our safety, it would be helpful if you could put Oscar into a different room."

Richards glared at Scott for a moment before relenting. He ordered the dog to his bed, and Oscar duly obliged, lifting his heavy bulk and padding out of the room.

Abby stood by the window and glanced out past the dirty net curtains, hoping the outlook was better than the room she stood in. A bleak and grey landscape stood beyond the property. Houses in the area were in dire need of a facelift and the road was littered with discarded rubbish.

She cast a cursory eye over the photos that lined the windowsill. Different images showed Richards in front of various bars and pubs, one arm draped over the shoulder of one friend or another, his other raising a pint glass in the air.

Abby sighed and turned back to Scott and Richards, notebook and pen in hand.

"What do you want to know?" Richards asked.

Scott said, "Where were you on Sunday night between six p.m. and midnight?"

"I was here watching TV, and I can tell you everything I watched."

"Anyone else with you?"

"Oscar." Richards smiled, pleased with his smug reply.

"You don't seem that surprised or upset about Linda's murder?"

Richards shrugged. "She's nothing to do with me anymore. If you think I killed her, then you're barking up the wrong tree." There was a measure of anger in his curt reply.

"But you displayed some aggressive tendencies towards her in the past. From our enquiries, I understand you may have assaulted her on more than one occasion?"

"So what? She was out of order. I'd had a bit to drink. I gave her a slap."

"That's assault in the eyes of the law."

"She didn't complain. I think she liked it. You know, the rough stuff."

Abby shook her head in a mixture of disbelief and anger as she observed Richards. He displayed an arrogance that riled her.

"The rough stuff?" Scott probed.

"Yeah. What the fuck are you doing here anyway?"

"Mr Richards. Whenever we investigate a violent assault or murder, it's standard procedure to question everyone connected to the victim. Partners, whether current or ex, can often provide us with vital information either as witnesses or suspects."

It was the last word that inflamed Richards; he pounded the armrests. "Don't try to fucking blame this on me! Why is it always the exes who get done?"

Scott goaded him further. "Because in our experience, they are often the ones who have the biggest grudge."

The two men stared at each other, Scott unperturbed, Richards incensed.

"Well, as I said, you're looking in the wrong place."

Scott changed tack. "Tell us about Linda. What was she like as a person?"

"She was okay, I guess. A bit of a slapper."

"Slapper?"

"Yeah, filthy fucking bitch, always wanting it. And not just your normal shit."

It was Scott's turn to sigh; he caught Abby rolling her eyes. "Could you elaborate?"

"Well, she wasn't the roll-on roll-off ferry type, if you get my drift."

Scott read between the lines as Richards continued.

"She couldn't get enough. She wanted it all the time. Always up for trying new things, new positions, and new toys. I'd be lying in bed and she'd be frigging herself off beside me. That's like a sex addiction thing, isn't it?"

"Do you know of anyone that may have wanted to harm her?"

"Listen, don't get me wrong. She was a slapper, but she wasn't a horrible person. She was a good mum to Shannon." Richards let out a small laugh. "Better parent than me. I was a useless dad. Me and her didn't work out, but I don't think she could have pissed off anyone enough for them to kill her."

"And did she meet anyone else whilst with you?" Scott knew the reply before it had left Richards's mouth.

"Take your pick. She loved the attention she got. She was forever sticking her tits out and winking as cars beeped at her."

"That must have annoyed you?"

"Wouldn't it you?"

"Enough to hurt her?" Scott asked.

"She was on these dating sites. She told me as much. I had a look on one, something like Hot Milfs, but I can't remember the name. I couldn't see her face, but I recognised her straight away."

"How?"

Richards stared at Scott in consternation. "Because of her tattoo, and well her...bits. It was definitely her."

The revelation that Linda was on another site unknown to them caused Scott to raise a brow.

Richards fell silent and dropped his head. "She was knocking someone else off. I found her in the sack with him."

"And that's when you assaulted her?"

Richards nodded unashamedly.

"Who was he? Had you seen him before?" Scott asked.

Richards shook his head.

"What happened when you found them?"

"I came home; it was dark. I went into the bedroom but didn't want to wake her. I saw her outline and then a second outline...and there she was, with him. I lost it and went mental. Everything after that was a blur. He legged it; she screamed the place down and..."

"You hit her," Abby spat out.

Richards fell silent and looked away.

"Did you get a look of him?" Scott asked.

"If I did I don't remember. Everything was a blur for the next few minutes. I remember he grabbed his clothes. He tried to rush past me but I managed to smack him around the face, and then I remember steaming towards the bed, wanting to throw the bitch out the window. Next thing I can remember is seeing her crumpled in a corner, holding her face and crying."

"Was he white, black, Asian?"

"White." Richards's eyes narrowed in reflection. "Dark, short hair. And butt fucking naked."

"What time was this?"

"Around two in the morning."

Scott folded his arms and slowly paced around the room, his eyes darting from one object to another. The sofas were worn, the carpet as threadbare as the one in the hallway. The surfaces carried a fine layer of dust, and bulky carrier bags sat stacked in one corner.

"You were working at the time?"

"Yeah, I was doing a bit of door work. Terry's bar in town. I'd knock off around one thirty a.m., but didn't always head home. I'd hang back for a couple of hours just to chill with some punters, or crash at a mate's house. Linda was usually asleep anyway, so there wasn't any point in going home."

Scott was familiar with Terry's bar. It was an illegal drinking establishment that had been shut down several times by the council.

"What made you go home on that occasion?"

Richards shrugged. "Dunno." He fell silent for a few moments. "I noticed that she wasn't gagging for it as much.

That's not like her. She'd always want it. I checked her phone a few days earlier and she'd been texting some guy, saying she was looking forward to getting him into her bed."

"Did you want to catch her?"

"Yeah. I wanted to fucking nail the pair."

"You did that," Abby muttered under her breath, as restlessness crept into her bones.

"Did you see much of her after you split?"

"Not really. I got the odd text off her about me not seeing Shannon. But we did our own thing. I offered for Shannon to come and stay with me occasionally, but Linda wasn't having it. She was worried Cujo would bite Shannon."

"Cujo?"

"Oscar. You never saw the film *Cujo*, from the eighties?"

Scott and Abby stared blankly at each other.

Scott asked, "Do you think the man in your bed was the married man she was allegedly involved with?"

"Aren't they all? I bet most of the punters on those sites are desperate blokes with wives that don't put out anymore. They must have thought Christmas had come early when they contacted Linda."

"And that must have upset you?"

"Who gives a fuck anymore? She moved on and found someone else, but that didn't last long either. She was never happy with her lot. She was always chasing the thrill."

20

Late afternoon fatigue appeared to rob the team of their enthusiasm as they gathered around the incident board. Whether it was due to a general malaise or a lack of progress on the investigation into Linda's death, Scott need to keep the team focused.

He began by updating the team on his and Abby's visits to question Linda's mum, Dalca and Richards. He pointed out a common pattern of fractured relationships that had blighted Linda's life. Dalca, Richards, and her mum were the tip of the iceberg.

Abby pressed home what a lowlife Richards appeared to be and noted that it would be worth uniform following up on the items she'd seen at the apartment, just in case they were stolen.

"Guv, the search for the missing items have drawn a blank," Mike said. "There's no sign of her shoes, skirt, or underwear."

Scott had expected that feedback. It was an extensive search area for the items. The theory now was that the missing items had been removed as trophies, or discarded elsewhere.

"I still believe there are remarkable similarities between our case and the one in Cardiff," Scott said. "The case file should be with us shortly, but I have little hope in solving it. Other than DNA evidence, they had no witnesses, no suspects, and they didn't find Daisy's shoes or underwear."

"Have we got an update on the DNA analysis?" asked Helen.

"Still waiting. I'll chase it up, but it will make our job both easier and harder if it connects the two cases."

Raj speculated on the possibility that someone might have tipped off Richards about the affair his wife was having. No one in the team could confirm who that might have been. Helen suggested someone may have overheard her at work talking about her love life. It wasn't uncommon in their experience for a victim to have been harassed, assaulted, or even murdered because of infatuation from a colleague. Scott knew what that felt like, having been on the receiving end of unwanted attention and blackmail from DCI Berry.

"That will be a new line of enquiry, Helen, her employers," he said. "We are picking apart her love life and forming a picture. We now need to explore the connections with work. It's a small firm, so everyone should know each other well. I can't imagine many secrets being kept hidden for long. Someone will know something."

Abby added, "Richards suggested that anyone who knew Linda well would have recognised her on the adult contact sites. As we know already, some images were full frontals. Others were discreet but features like her tattoo would have made her identifiable to those who knew her. In fact, Richards was blunter than that. His suggestion was that anyone who had been intimate with her would have recognised her by her genitalia."

Raj and Mike exchanged a discreet smile that threatened to explode into raucous laughter. They were acting like naughty schoolboys who had just discovered the centrefold in a Playboy magazine.

"Don't forget, we may never know the full extent of the contact she had with men through the site," Scott said. "During our visit, Richards explained that Linda used to go out once a month to supposedly meet up with friends in town for drinks but wouldn't explain her reasons for rolling in at breakfast time. It's possible she was meeting men, whose identities will remain unknown."

Abby ran a hand through her hair and blew out her cheeks. "Needle in a haystack springs to mind? To that list we can add the married man she had an affair with, the man Richards found her in bed with, and Leo's father."

There was a consensus of nods from the others.

Scott said, "I will contact the psychological profiler for a different angle and a clean perspective on what we are doing."

There was a collective groan from the others.

"Guv, we need old-school policing here, not psycho, mumbo-jumbo bollocks," Mike said.

Scott raised his hand to quiet the ripples of laughter. "Okay, okay. Glad you say it as you see it, Mike, but we need all the help we can. Listen, if the profiler gives us nothing of interest, we've not lost anything, have we?"

Mike viewed him with suspicion. "I know you're into it, guv, but it doesn't wash with me."

"Yes, Mike. I know what you're like. You'd much rather walk around the streets smacking nine bells out of the informants, the pushers, and dealers, and any lowlife pond scum to get your answers."

"No harm with that, guv," Mike teased.

With nothing further to add, Scott instructed the team to knock off and get an early night.

"I FEEL SORRY FOR LINDA," Abby said, as she fumbled for her keys beside her car.

Scott nodded and stared off into the distance.

She added, "Part of me thinks she was desperate for love, and the other part makes me think she didn't know what she wanted. As if searching for the missing magic bullet, the attention and sex filled a void in her life."

"Possibly," Scott replied, as he watched two officers set off in a patrol car. He recognised the driver and gave her a wave as she passed. "She lived life on the edge and craved a connection. In a way she was being used, but she was also using men she met to satisfy something in her. She wasn't into vanilla sex that's for sure."

"You're not wrong there, guv. I nearly died of embarrassment when Richards went into graphic detail about Linda's bits." She shuddered at the thought.

"What are you up to tonight? Are you in with the kids?" Scott asked.

Abby smiled. "Yep. We are making home-made pizzas tonight. I'm just going to pop into Sainsbury's and pick up ham, pineapple chunks, pepperoni, and chicken. Why don't you join us? The kids would love to see you. Jonathon is coming over later, so it will be fun. I'll make you my mean hot chocolate to warm you up, with added galaxy chunks thrown in for good measure."

Scott loved the idea, and envied Abby's opportunity to have a family night in. He groaned inwardly not wishing to spoil Abby's enthusiasm.

"I'd love to, but I'm meeting Cara for dinner tonight. How about another time? And I'll shout you a load of Domino pizzas? All kids love a Domino." He laughed.

It was Abby's turn to groan. "That sounds so much easier than making them. But the kids are excited and that's the main thing."

Casa Don Carlos was a small Spanish restaurant tucked away deep in The Lanes. The family-friendly restaurant was full and buzzing by the time Scott arrived. It was a great venue that offered an authentic tapas menu that made you feel like you were in Spain. Many of the locals were repeat customers who swore that it was some of the best tapas outside Barcelona and beat a lot within that city.

With great food and even better service, it was a favourite with Scott. Cara sat in the corner, working her way through a large glass of white wine when she spotted Scott striding towards her. She greeted him with a slow smile that suggested it wasn't her first glass either.

"Sorry I'm late, lover. I needed to finish the briefing. It looks like you started without me?" He flicked his head at the half-empty wine bottle.

"Hmm, probably. It's going down a little too easy, so we need some food before I fall off this chair," she slurred.

Scott took a few moments to kiss Cara softly on the lips. Her eyes, showing hunger to explore his mouth further, captivated and pulled him in. They were a deep brown – the colour of the earth after torrential rains. But there was something else in them, something glistening. They shimmered like old copper pennies being examined under a light. Cara exuded a warmth and magnetism that swallowed Scott's attention.

Dressed in skin-tight denim jeans, knee-length black boots, and a thin jumper, Cara's form knocked him for six, and he thanked the universe for bringing her into his life.

"Did I tell you that I love you?" he whispered.

Cara rolled her eyes and appeared to think it through. She kept him waiting a few moments. "I think you may have done occasionally. And I love you just as much. But can we order some food?"

"You and your food. I thought I was bad but you're terrible."

They ordered paella for two, deep-fried whitebait, grilled squid, chickpeas with spinach, Spanish sausage cooked in wine, grilled prawns and home-made chicken-and Serrano-ham croquettes.

Tonight, was about relaxing and enjoying each other's company, and the restaurant was the perfect setting for that. It carried the Spanish vibes of relaxed and laid-back. No one was in a hurry to leave, nor was anyone in a hurry to be served. It was the perfect place to unwind after a few hectic days.

They had decided not to talk about work for a change, so Scott didn't mention how his current investigation was proceeding, and how the lack of progress frustrated him. Cara in return hadn't touched on her work following a house fire, and some suspicious deaths. They could talk about those another day.

"I think your eyes are bigger than your belly," Cara said, as she scanned the tapas plates that took up every square inch of the table. She had left the whitebait and grilled squid to Scott. Having tried squid before, she had decided that it tasted like a glorified rubber band. Instead, she enjoyed the prawns and chicken croquettes, and tucked in to their paella.

A break from work was the tonic they both needed. Tonight, their jobs faded into the background. They were nothing more than a normal couple, like so many others who were enjoying a warm, romantic meal together.

Two hours later, they left the restaurant. The cold onshore breeze blew right through Cara's sweater. She bent her head and closed her lashes weighed down with mascara to keep out the salty sting. The chill of the night air cut through her skinny jeans as she snuggled in closer to Scott. Her hair fell loose about her face, tousled, and tangled.

Moisture clung heavy in the air, heralding the likelihood of rain closing in on them. They quickened their pace and headed for the car park.

21

Her cries went unnoticed, her pleas unheard.

No doors.

No windows.

No way out.

Every minute felt like hours. She could hear a clock tick close by. With effort, she opened her weary eyes but saw nothing. Darkness enveloped her, trapping her in a cocoon of hell. Maybe she had imagined the clock... yet its echoes penetrated the stillness of the air.

Looking around, she could see an indefinite expansion of pure dark space. No light. No shadows. Only different shades of blackness. Though there appeared to be nothing but open space around her, she felt the feeling of suffocation, like her lungs were caving in. She was trapped, imprisoned in her own mind. She could move nothing but her eyes; her mind raced whilst every muscle stayed still.

There was nothing for company other than her heartbeat and rancid breath. The smell of her piss and shit blended into the stale, pungent smells that hung in the air.

Every time she shifted the wire screeched; its shrill echo cut into her. Her skin was sickly and pallid, stretched over her stark bones. She hadn't eaten or drunk much for a week – maybe longer, she couldn't be certain. Her feet were bare and grubby, and all she wore over her frail body was a set of ragged robes soiled by her own bodily waste.

She'd never felt so alone.

Fear replaced tiredness, weakness and surrender. Desperate to be heard, she cried out once more, but nothing other than a faint whisper escaped from her dry throat. Sadness welled deep within and she cried, but no tears fell. She had nothing left.

Rats scurried beneath her feet. At first she'd been scared of them, but they now offered her a perverse comfort. She wasn't alone.

The cold of the winter's night didn't penetrate this deep down. The small gas heater had lost its warm orange glow hours ago but heat remained, stroking her clammy skin.

He's never let the gas run out before, she thought. *Will it make any difference if he comes? He'll only offer a few scraps of food and some Ribena, things my body rejects. Why I don't know.*

Why me? How long will he keep me here? Why is he keeping me here? Someone must be looking for me by now.

Her eyes felt heavy, and the feeling of hunger left her. She succumbed to tiredness once again.

THURSDAY NIGHT WAS the start of the weekend for many, and this week was no different. The pub was busy. A cacophony of multiple conversations reverberated around him, of which he grabbed snippets. One man moaned to his friend about being given extra shifts at work; another group discussed holiday locations for the summer; and others murmured quietly whilst sipping their pints.

He had been to this pub three times already, so was glad it was busy tonight. It was smaller than the others that he'd been to, which meant there was a greater risk of being spotted. He never went to the same pub more than once every few weeks. He didn't want to be spotted as a regular, nor did he want to become a familiar face that customers and bar staff would recognise. Dipping in and out of pubs meant he remained invisible. He would order a pint and then melt into the crowd before bar staff had a good opportunity to take in his features.

He liked this pub. The barmaid was just as he had remembered her on his last visit. She looked much better than her profile pictures. They had exchanged pleasantries online; the conversations became more risqué when they exchanged photographs. He knew what she was hiding beneath her skinny jeans, white Converse trainers, and a simple, white long-sleeved T-shirt. Oh yes, he *loved* what she hid beneath her clothes.

The pictures she'd sent had blown his mind. Just thinking about them made him erect. A pierced bar went through each of her nipples, and a ring went through her pierced clitoral hood. She was filthy. He smiled to himself as he imagined men choking on their pints if they knew that the woman they were having a cheeky banter with across the bar was a filthy whore.

Luckily, she hadn't recognised him. He had chosen another member of the staff to serve him, which allowed him to watch her from a discreet distance. He loved her European accent. She had come to Brighton from a place called Prienai in Lithuania seven months ago. The UK had been part of her travels after she'd moved through Poland, Germany, France, Belgium, and the Netherlands. She had spoken about wanting to experience life, and how there were very few people, and men, where she lived. But she enjoyed fucking men, and borrowing money off them with no intention of paying it back. She was just a whore who exploited a man's weakness.

No one will miss her, he thought. She had moved around so much that it was unlikely anyone could have kept track of her. She told him that her father had passed away some time ago, and that her mother had brought her up. Her mother was a disciplinarian, but Katrina was a rebel. Like water and oil, they didn't mix.

Katrina was just another migrant, working in various pubs and restaurants to fund her travels. She had already spoken about leaving in a few weeks – her destination, Greece. If he didn't act now he would lose her.

He faced a dilemma; he needed to get rid of Emma first. She had been a waste of time. She had promised so much and delivered so little. It had incensed him; she talked the talk but she was a tease. She needed to be punished for that. He hated women taking advantage of him, always had. Emma had let him down. Now he needed to figure out a way to get rid of her. His efforts to conceal the last body had been futile, and had only bought him limited time. If he was to cover his tracks properly, he would need to find a better way of stashing the body.

Perhaps burying them in a deeper pit would work better? But that would require more effort, and the longer I hang around, the more chance I have of being discovered. There are no lakes close by and dumping a body in the sea is a definite no-no, because the tide would pull them back in again. Decisions, decisions.

His mind raced as he considered his options.

HER MIND FLOPPED between surrender and fear. Her thoughts spun like a vortex. Moments of grey blended with white noise rushed through her and wore down her senses. Her awareness had been weakened. If she clung tight enough, she could rest on the narrow crescent platform. Sleep and fatigue willed her to rest, but the cable tied around her neck cut into her red, bleeding skin. Each movement stung like lemon juice had been rubbed into her wounds.

Her body started the slow process of shutting down – the body's natural attempts at self-preservation – robbing her of her senses. She'd lost count of the number of times she'd jolted in her sleep and her body had rolled perilously close to the edge of the platform and the sheer drop beyond.

Why hasn't he come today? I'm getting cold again.

22

Scott let out a muffled groan from beneath the bedcovers. He peered over the top as if he was hiding from someone. Officially, it was his rest day, but a call had been arranged with Cardiff police to discuss their cold case. The clock said six-thirty a.m., yet his body suggested it was earlier.

Cara's warm body was entwined in the covers. Scott curled in behind and wrapped his arms around her. She wiggled against him when his chest hair tickled her. As he buried his face in her neck, his body twitched in response to her.

"I need to get up, babes. I need to head in. I've got an important call to make."

Cara groaned and pulled his arms tighter to her, a silent response to his words.

"It's your day off. Abby's in. Can't she take care of it?"

"I know. I'm sorry; I'll be back as quick as I can." It wasn't the exact truth, but he didn't want to upset her further.

"Well then, let her handle it. I took the day off to spend it with you. I thought we could stay in bed most of the morning and then grab a late lunch. I promise, you'll have worked up a hunger by then." She twisted her hand behind her body and grabbed his groin.

"Will you stop it?" he teased. "You always want it. Anyone would think you've been a nun for most of your life and now you need to make up for lost time!"

"What can I say," she purred. "You've awoken something in me. I've never felt so alive and sexy in my life."

"Glad I could help."

Scott peeled himself away from her and padded through the chill of the morning before grabbing a shower. Cara fell asleep.

WITH THE TEAM busy following up leads and double-checking witness statements, there was little else Scott could do to progress the case. They didn't have a firm suspect. DNA results were taking longer than expected, and he had a local councillor looking for answers that Scott couldn't give him.

Scott had called DI Eddie Hanlon from Cardiff CID thirty minutes ago, but Hanlon was tied up in a meeting and would return Scott's call as soon as he was free. In the meantime, Scott reviewed the notes on the system. The description of the man outside The Greys Pub intrigued him. As part of an investigation, Scott would always turn the spotlight on friends and family first.

The problem was Linda had many men in her in life. Richards, Dalca, a married man, her date, plus many unknowns from the adult contact sites.

Scott's mobile ringing interrupted his thoughts.

He answered it. “Hello?”

“DI Eddie Hanlon here, sorry for not being available when you called. I understand you want to talk about a cold case of ours?”

“That’s fine. We need your thoughts on a case we’re dealing with now.”

“Yes, so I gather. It sounds like a meaty one. Rather you than me,” Hanlon joked.

“Yes, I don’t envy us at the moment. Anyway, other than what’s in the case file for your stranger rape murder, is there anything else you can think of that might help us?” Scott added his thoughts about the two cases being connected and the lack of leads in both cases.

There was a lengthy pause followed by a sigh. “Well, it’s not uncommon to come across a stranger rape, but very few lead to a murder. That’s the bit we focused on. It carried the same hallmarks as your case. Daisy Callaghan used a couple of online adult apps to make friends, and to see if any of those would become more than just friends.”

“And how did that work out?”

“We recovered her phone and there were messages from men who had contacted her, and a few women, to be honest. We traced quite a few who had contacted her by text and WhatsApp using their own mobiles. It eliminated them from our investigations. There were five we could not trace. Two were pay-as-you-go numbers, the others were email addresses. We traced IP addresses, but they led to public places, like coffee shops and high street stores. Anyone standing in proximity to those locations could tap into free Wi-Fi networks.”

“It sounds like your case hit the same barriers as ours.”

Hanlon didn’t agree or disagree. “We had one line of

enquiry based on one of those pay-as-you-go numbers that offered potential. Daisy exchanged several messages with an unknown male. The person had deleted the earlier conversations because there were only two messages from Daisy, but it was clear they'd had prior contact."

Hanlon carried on describing how Daisy had sent a message saying, "I really enjoyed our evening last night, my head is still pounding this morning. When will I see you again?" To which the unknown male had replied, "I'm not sure. I'm not over that way. I was only there for the weekend. Maybe I can come over and see you in a few weeks' time?" Daisy's reply to that had been, "Okay."

Scott rolled a pen through his fingers, desperate to pick up on anything of interest. "What about her movements in the weeks prior to her death?"

"We covered that, too. I think most of it is in the report. We did an extensive trawl of CCTV. We found her at several locations in and around Cardiff Central. The Great Western and the Prince of Wales, specifically. Both are Wetherspoon pubs. She was seen at local clubs and other bars. She was a creature of habit."

"Anything stand out?" As Scott asked, Abby poked her head around his door. Scott gestured silently for her to grab a seat opposite him and he put on his phone on loudspeaker.

"We picked up on some pub CCTV footage." Hanlon said. "She talked to a few people. Some footage was too grainy, so we went back to those pubs frequently over the course of a few weeks, and the persistence paid off. We tracked down several of the people she'd spoken to. Again, nothing untoward, and I eliminated them from the investigation. To be honest, it's hard to trawl through the footage. We have so many hen parties and stag parties that travel from all over the country. They roam the streets at weekends. The perp could have been a local or someone from out-of-town."

The enormity of the investigation sent shivers through Scott. Abby tutted.

"Have you had any other similar cases since then?" Scott asked Hanlon.

"Nope. Nothing matching that MO."

The conversation offered nothing new regarding his current investigation, but it had shed light on the circumstances and background surrounding the death of Daisy Callaghan.

"I CAN TELL YOU'RE DISAPPOINTED," Abby commented as she got out of the car.

"That obvious?" Scott said.

"You said fuck all in the car, and your lips moving silently as if you were talking to yourself was a giveaway."

"You don't miss a thing, do you?"

"I learnt from the best." She winked in reply, as she opened the door to their next destination and stepped in to reception.

Box K4 Software Solutions was situated on the Hyde Business Park, towards the northeast of town, skirted on three sides by open land and forest. With nothing other than the odd delivery van and a passing car, it was in marked contrast to the hustle and bustle of the city centre.

Scott hoped that the visit would open the case and present a different perspective on Linda's life. Aluna Yafai had been her closest friend at Box K4. But before Scott approached her, he needed to build a picture of the company and the key players. Scott hoped Aluna might know who Richards had found in bed with Linda, as well as provide new insight into her private life.

Scott and Abby were led upstairs to some carpeted offices at the back of the building. They were shown into an office with deep-pile red carpet. A large, transparent glass desk held two twenty-four-inch computer monitors fixed to one side, and a simple white keyboard occupied the centre of the desk.

"Minimal to say the least," Scott murmured as they both stared at the desk. There were no filing trays, penholders, nothing to spoil the clean-cut lines. The rest of the room carried the same styling. A bookshelf in one corner had just a few books on each shelf; three prints occupied one wall and a whiteboard occupied the other. They refused the receptionist's offer of refreshments and were offered a seat.

Minutes later, a man in a grey suit with an open-neck shirt strode in, extending his hand. "Sorry to keep you waiting. I'm Christopher Weatherford, managing director and owner of Box 4 Software Solutions."

Another man in a red-checked open shirt and blue jeans accompanied Weatherford. He had tightly cropped hair and a stubbly beard, both of which had patches of grey. His face was long. His blue eyes darted between both visitors.

"This is Adam Hobday, he's –"

Before Weatherford could finish the introductions, Abby interrupted with a firm tone, "And what do you do here, Mr Hobday?"

Hobday glanced between the officers and Weatherford, who had a hint of annoyance on his face at being interrupted. Weatherford retrieved a folder from one shelf.

"I...I'm a freelance IT software consultant specialising in Java applications with Spring Framework."

Hobday stared at Abby. She held his gaze. Though she didn't have a clue what any of that meant, she wouldn't admit it. She glanced at Scott and knew he was holding in a laugh.

Scott introduced himself and Abby, as Weatherford took his seat across the table to them. Weatherford handed the file to Hobday and the consultant hastily exited the room before he could be asked any further questions.

Weatherford shifted in his leather chair. "Adam works on projects for us as a freelancer. We have a few we send out to client sites across the country, Glasgow, Cardiff, Leeds, London, that sort of thing. We don't always have the expertise in-house, so rather than lose the business, we subcontract parts out. They do charge a fortune for what is a very lucrative career."

Scott remained silent.

Weatherford continued. "I understand you're investigating the death of one of our employees. We are deeply saddened by the news. It came as quite a shock."

As the man ran a hand through his immaculately combed hair, his concern and upset were clear to Scott. Weatherford had a distinctive dimple in his chin and cheeks when he smiled, both of which were not evident with his solemn expression.

"What does your business do?" Scott asked.

It took a moment for Weatherford to compose himself again. "We design bespoke business applications, bespoke CRM systems, handle software, hardware integration, data migration, legacy software modernisation, and offer software consultancy, both in-house and through a network of freelance consultants, Adam being one of them."

The description was lost on both Abby and Scott as they exchanged the briefest of glances. It was Abby's turn to hide her smile.

"Did Mr Hobday know Linda?" Scott asked.

"I imagine so. Most of our freelancers spend time here for meetings and so forth."

"We'll need his contacts details then, as we need to speak to everyone who knew her."

"Of course, Inspector."

"What can you tell us about Linda?"

"She was a bright, bubbly person. Always the first to laugh at a joke. She was hard-working and, as you know, she had two young children to look after. I imagine it wasn't easy for her to juggle work and being a single parent."

Abby made notes while Scott led the questioning. She glanced around to see small trophies on one shelf. She couldn't make out the inscriptions from where she was sitting, but they looked like industry awards of some sort.

"Did you know much about her life outside of work?" Scott asked.

Weatherford shook his head. "I'm only concerned about my employees' lives if it affects their work."

"How about colleagues? Did she get on with many of them?"

"She had a friendly word with everyone she came across in her work. She never had a bad word to say about anyone. She was friendly with Aluna Yafai, who's another technical support assistant. They sat near each other, so spent a lot of time together. And if I'm honest, they spent far too much time talking than working."

Scott told Weatherford that they'd like to speak to Aluna, and he obliged by calling his secretary to arrange it.

"And where were you last Sunday evening, Mr Weatherford?" Scott asked.

Weatherford was clearly taken aback by his directness. He stared open-mouthed for a few seconds longer than he needed to.

"Am I under suspicion or something?"

"It depends if you have something to hide, Mr Weatherford. But it's a standard question we ask of anyone who knew or met Linda regularly. What is more important to us is accounting for the final hours and days whilst Linda was alive." Scott's tone was firm and sharp.

Weatherford shrugged. "I was at home with my wife. You're more than welcome to ask her," he replied dryly.

"And when was the last time you saw Linda?"

"That would have been Friday, when she left work. You can check the electronic log if you want to. Every single employee, including me, must swipe in and swipe out. Linda would have left around five-thirty, but I can check that for you, and I left a little before nine."

"That's late. Is it a common thing?"

Weatherford nodded and shrugged a shoulder. "It is when you're the managing director. It's a very competitive industry we're in, and if I could work seven days a week, I would. Though I doubt my wife would let me," he joked.

Scott nodded but offered no response. He was analysing the man's facial characteristics and movements. Normally he'd look at Weatherford's eye movements, to understand how he processed information. But on this occasion, Weatherford was looking straight at Scott. On occasion, he diverted his attention to Abby to see what she was writing.

"One line of enquiry that we are following up is that she was involved with a married man –" Abby began.

Before she could finish, Weatherford sat up, alarmed. He held his hands out in surrender. "Whoa, whoa, backup a sec. If you're implying anything untoward, then you're mistaken." He shook his head in protest. "I'm married, not always happily, but nevertheless, married."

"I wasn't implying anything, Mr Weatherford," Abby said. "I was merely asking whether you knew anything about it. Maybe she was involved with another married employee within your company?"

Weatherford offered nothing more than a shake of his head.

Scott informed him that officers would be arriving that afternoon to interview members of staff, and that he would need details of those who were not in the office today. Weatherford said he would make space available to accommodate the officers and get those details.

As soon as Aluna Yafai arrived outside waiting to be seen, they concluded their interview with Mr Weatherford.

23

Weatherford brought Aluna into his office and left, to afford her some privacy with Scott and Abby.

She was a slim, Anglo-African woman with a pale-brown complexion, and shoulder-length dark-brown hair that was fashionably shaped in long ringlets. Her strong and angular features were offset by an attractive, blemish-free complexion that accentuated her youthfulness. She wore an off-the-shoulder T-shirt, jeans, and Converse trainers. Scott put her in her late twenties.

Her welcoming smile was soon replaced by sadness. Sorrow clouded her face. Her eyes welled as she brought her hand to her lips. "I understand you want to see me?"

Scott nodded at Abby, suggesting that she take the lead.

Abby leant forward on her elbows, softening her expression. "We are investigating the murder of Linda Allen. We understand from Mr Weatherford that you two were close?"

Aluna offered nothing more than a nod as she fought to

compose herself. "I still can't believe she's gone. Why would anyone do that to her? She wouldn't hurt a fly."

"We are looking at all aspects of her life, but it's her personal life we are most interested in. I understand she was meeting men through online adult contact sites. Do you know much about that?"

Aluna's eyes widened. "Do you think it's one of them?"

"It seems a distinct possibility that whoever she met may have been responsible for her death. Do you know much about the people she contacted?"

"Not really, to be honest. She put in the ads and attached some saucy photographs of herself. She was like that, extroverted with sex. It seemed to be her favourite topic, and whenever she met someone, and had it...She went into a lot of detail, if you know what I mean?"

"Did she talk about the ads with anyone else? Perhaps someone at work who may have overheard your conversations?"

Aluna shook her head. "Definitely not work. We used to whisper about it in the ladies, as you do. She swore me to secrecy."

"Are you sure no one else knew?"

The woman thought for a few moments. "Jackie, her neighbour. That was the only other person."

Abby continued. "Did she talk about the type of guys she contacted? Were any names mentioned?"

Aluna was unable to elaborate on that point other than to say Linda had been inundated with replies. Some were polite, others obscene, sending her pictures of their genitalia in various states of arousal.

"Did it bother her?" Abby asked.

"Oh, God no. If anything, it turned her on. I think she

loved sex. She couldn't get enough. I think we can safely say she had a high sex drive, and wasn't the type to enjoy straightforward sex, but she needed money..."

Abby narrowed her eyes. "Did she ever charge men for sex?"

"Not as far as I know. But they'd spend their money when she was with them. And then there was *him*."

"Him?"

"She had a brief relationship with someone, I'm not sure who, but then she had Leo, and he gave her a lot of cash."

Abby glanced at Scott as more pieces of the jigsaw fell in place.

The woman's hands flew to her neck. "Oh, shit, I swore I would tell no one."

"Are you telling us that she had a relationship with someone who wanted her to have a baby, and in return he provided for her financially?"

"No. She didn't go into detail. Nor did I ask. The less I knew the better. As far as I know, he wasn't interested in a long-term relationship with her. Unfortunately, it all went horribly wrong for her..."

"Wrong?" Abby asked.

Aluna nodded. "After Leo was born, she loved the baby too much. She couldn't bear to give him up. Her mum knew all about it, and that's why they stopped talking. She got her money, and she got to keep Leo. Whether the guy was pleased about that or not, I'm not sure."

The revelation came as a surprise for both officers.

Abby sensed a breakthrough. With urgency in her tone, she asked, "Did she ever mention his name? Was he married, single?"

"She never said."

"Could it have been an employee from here?"

She shrugged. "Your guess is as good as mine. He could have been from here, he could have been someone she met online, or he could have been someone she met in a bar."

Scott's mind raced. Linda had hidden the identity of the father well. Her closest friends and family weren't privy to the information.

"Did she mention anything about the date last Sunday evening?" Abby asked.

"She was excited, that's for sure. He seemed to press the right buttons, and the conversation between them was racy. Linda felt they already knew each other. They seemed to connect. Linda had bought a new outfit, new underwear....she was always prepared, and new shoes. Jackie would do her hair...She was going all out to impress him."

SCOTT AND ABBY were discussing the case over a sandwich in his office when the call came through. A member of Matt's forensic team delivered the breakthrough they needed. Until this point, a lack of forensics had been hampering his investigation, and they'd had to resort to good old-fashioned policing to progress the case.

Scott's face lit up as he listened to the feedback from the officer. "Are you absolutely sure? Okay, can you cross-check against the mouth swabs we've taken so far and update me? Thanks."

Right before Scott hung up, a jolt of excitement surged through him.

Abby shot him an inquisitive stare. She wiped her mouth and put her Diet Coke can down. "Well?"

"Forensics has confirmed a DNA match between our case and Cardiff. I knew it." Scott punched the air. "He's done this before. The duct tape used to bind Linda came back negative. It contained her hair and skin fibres."

"Fuck, that's brilliant. Any hits on the database?"

Scott shook his head. "That would make it too easy for us. We still need to find him. We've taken samples from Richards, Dalca, and Weatherford so far. Forensics will cross-reference them. Do me a favour, update the rest of the team and give DI Hanlon in Cardiff a call. I'll update the super."

HER FRAIL limp body had all but given up when light flooded the chamber. The shards of brilliance punctured her eyes like tiny needles. She squinted and turned her face from the source.

Her body emaciated, weak and dirty, she resembled a destitute and homeless soul abandoned by society, robbed of life and love.

He shone his torch on her face as he removed the steel cable from around her neck. Her eyelids clamped shut, to block out the worst of the pain. His hands caressed her body. He fondled her breasts, clearly enjoying the sensation of rolling her nipples through his fingers. She jolted at the violation, too weak to turn and fend him off. His touch repulsed her. Her mind fought to distract her, sending her consciousness off to a sunny beach where she could hear the sea lapping the shore, and children laughing as they splashed through the surf.

She felt a hand creep between her legs, violating her

further, exploring in a way that only a couple in love would. Every time he penetrated her she tried to cry out, but her throat was too dry to make a sound.

He smiled as he stepped away and retrieved a small bottle of water and a slice of bread from a carrier bag he'd brought with him. She took a few sips of the water. With her lips cracked, her mouth blistered, and her throat tinder dry, each drop felt like a large stone as she attempted to swallow.

"You are such a disappointment. I thought you would be fun. You fucking teased me. The pictures you sent me were of someone else, you lying, filthy whore."

She shook her head. "Pleeease...Pleeease let me go. I...just...want...to...go...home."

"You haven't got a fucking home. No one will miss you. No one is looking for you."

She pleaded again but was cut short when he launched a ferocious attack on her, punching her in the face. Speckles of blood erupted from her lips, the tiny winces of noise she made echoing around the chamber. He covered her face with the empty carrier bag and tightened it around her neck as he continued to pummel her. His venom, his wrath and anger spewed out with every punch.

Her limp body collapsed in a heap on the platform. He removed the bag to see her bloodied and battered face. With one final glance, he stomped on her face; a sickening crack sound bounced around the confined space.

All the while, he became more aroused. He wasn't sure whether it was from touching her or beating her. Whatever it was, he enjoyed the feeling and took great pleasure in relieving himself over her broken body before securing the cable around her neck and leaving her once again.

His prized possessions had become the sole focus of his attention, gnawing away at him day and night, like a rat chewing through cable. Whenever he closed his eyes, his thoughts drifted back to the special gifts he had hidden away.

He'd promised his wife he wouldn't do it again, but there was a magnetic attraction that pulled him back every time. The buzz, the excitement, and the sordid pleasures he gained were like a drug. Addictive, consuming, and dangerous. He would often wait for Minu to be out or busy before he crept into the garage to entertain himself.

The shoe and underwear excited him. Every time he took them out of the bag, he felt like a child unwrapping a birthday present. His eyes grew wide and excited, his heart pounded, and his groin twitched.

Today was no different. As he wrapped the knickers around his cock, ecstasy washed through him. He clenched his jaw tight as he fantasised about the woman who had been wearing them.

His wife had never been like this. She preferred straightforward sex, which left him wanting. He would spend many nights on porn websites long after she had gone to bed. The expectation had been there when they had met. The sex was good if a little straightforward, but she had said the right things. She'd spoken frequently about wanting to try different things to please him.

They had been nothing but empty words, spoken in the heat of the moment. They were married now. Apart from a flagging, if non-existent, sex life, their relationship was good. They got on well, had a good social life, and they supported each other. Talking about their sex life was something neither did, regarding it as a taboo subject.

Wrapped up in his desires, he didn't hear Minu creep up behind him.

"You are a fucking bastard!" she screamed. Her face contorted in anger and revulsion as she stared at her husband stood there with his clothes around his ankles, naked and embarrassed.

His mouth dropped open, but no words would come. She had caught him once like this before. On that occasion, she had threatened to throw him out. He had pleaded and begged for a second chance, fearful of how his family and community would react.

On that occasion, the underwear had belonged to a married woman he had met through a dating site called Illicit Affairs. He had kept her soiled underwear as a souvenir.

"Who is she?" she spat as she lunged at him, pushing him backwards. "Who?"

He stood there, head bowed, his hands covering his groin in embarrassment.

Minu circled him and looked him up and down, disgust etched deep in the lines on her face. Fiery anger burnt in her eyes.

Whatever he would say would seem weak. "Minu, it's not like that. Please you have to understand. I swear I don't know who these belong to. I found them on the road." As the words tripped from his tongue, he knew it sounded pathetic – even worse, desperate.

"I want you gone from here," Minu said, as she turned and walked out.

24

Mike tapped away at his keyboard. His face was puffy and red, his eyes just as bad. He'd slept badly after a Friday night of drinking local brews at the Evening Star. He'd succumbed to the Dark Star favourite known as the crème brûlée, often dubbed a dessert in a glass with its vanilla and caramel undertones. Seven pints later, he'd staggered out of the pub and found his way home.

He groaned as Helen walked over to her desk.

"I hoped no one would be in for ages," he mumbled.

Helen tutted. "How many?" she asked, as she threw her jacket over the back of her chair.

"Don't ask and I won't lie."

Helen laughed as she headed for the coffee maker. She returned with a steaming, hot coffee. "Two sugars," she said with a saucy wink. "And don't let the guv see you like that, or he'll give you a right rollicking."

Mike mumbled something under his breath before

returning to his review of the incident that had occurred during the night.

"Anything of interest?" Helen asked, as she dropped a green-tea bag into her mug of boiling water.

Mike looked up and tipped his head in her direction. "Well, anything is more interesting than watching you make a cup of pond water."

"It's healthy. And you and healthy don't go in the same sentence." Helen cast him a disparaging look.

"It's mainly domestics. The usual bunch of fights in town for a Friday night. But we did have one call that uniform are following up on that may be of interest to us. A man followed a woman down Florence Road. The suspect was behind her for about fifteen minutes and gaining ground. She ran, and he pursued her. She screamed as he caught up with her. That seemed to be enough to scare him and he ran off."

"And the female?"

"She went to the nearest house and hammered down the door."

"Description?"

"Not much. Too dark. Assailant was IC1, medium height and build, wearing a black hoodie, and dark jeans."

Helen rolled her eyes. "That narrows it down."

"Always. What did you do last night? Anything exciting? Like make nettle soup, or discovered another use for a used green-tea bag?"

Helen made a mock gasp. "You're a cheeky shit." She grabbed a pencil from her desk and threw it at him. "You're making me out to be a commune loving, hippy chick who lives off the land. Just because I drink herbal teas and like couscous?"

Mike choked on his coffee. "There you go. I rest my case. Couscous! That's bloody rabbit food. They should ban it on health grounds."

"Don't tell me, you think a pie and chips, a Ginsters pasty, a fry-up, and half a gallon of beer are better, healthier options?"

Mike threw his arms in the air. "Nothing wrong with any of that. Good traditional English fayre. Staples for the working man."

"You really talk shit sometimes, Mike."

"Well?"

"Well, what?"

"What did you do last night, Helen?"

"If you must know, Mike, I went to the theatre in Eastbourne with a friend. We saw *La Traviata*, one of Verdi's greatest operas. It's a love story shrouded in sacrifice and misunderstanding, set in French society in the eighteen fifties."

"Oh, for fuck's sake. Don't go cultural on me again." Mike snorted, as he got up to refill his coffee.

Helen muttered something under her breath about Mike being un-cultured.

Adam Hobday made it clear to Scott that he didn't understand why he'd needed to be interviewed as part of the investigation. He reminded them that he'd mentioned that he knew Linda Allen, as did most of the employees at Box K4, but that was as far as it went. He continued to insist that he'd never socialised with her or met her outside the office environment. Reluctantly, he had agreed to meet with Scott and Abby at the offices he rented in town.

His objection to meeting the officers had piqued Scott's interest. It wasn't uncommon for people to be defensive when asked to an interview, as if agreeing would be an admission of guilt.

Hobday rented an office in a Regus building in the centre of town. Scott and Abby found his name on the company list in the unmanned reception and made their way up to the second floor. His office was on a corridor of identical-looking rooms. They all had a brown door and smoked glassed windows, with a discreet, silver doorplate announcing the name of each company. There was a mixture of companies that offered anything from accountancy, through to software consultancy, to travel, and business services.

Hobday sat behind a solitary desk, off to one side of the room. Filing cabinets and a large whiteboard occupied the remaining space, with a few guest chairs in front of the desk.

He was dressed casually in a pale-blue, open-neck shirt and cream chinos, with brown suede loafers. Though casual, there was an air of affluence about the way he dressed.

"Thank you for taking the time to see us," Scott offered.

"I didn't think I had much choice..." he replied sheepishly, his eyes reluctant to linger on either of the two officers. "I can spare you about thirty minutes, if that's okay? I have a conference call that I need to prepare for at midday."

"We won't take up too much of your time."

Scott had sensed a slight edginess to the man yesterday, and it continued today. Despite having the air of confidence and looking the part, his overall mannerisms were at odds with his persona. There was uncertainty, or perhaps fear in Hobday. A hidden anxiety manifesting itself through the narrowing and shiftiness in his eyes. A general fidgeting that Scott noticed, as Hobday clicked his pen rapidly. It was a behaviour that Abby had picked up on, too.

"How can I help?" Hobday asked.

Scott said, "How long have you freelanced for Box K4?"

The directness of his question appeared to unnerve Hobday, as he licked his lips and averted his gaze to the window.

He's buying time.

"I...I can't be certain without checking my files, but at least the past two years. At first it was the odd project, but more recently, I've been working with them every month."

"And does that involve being at their offices every month?"

"Yes, I would say so. With us being so close, I find it makes the working relationship far more harmonious. In our industry we work remotely, and much can be done virtually. It's refreshing to not be cooped up in this office."

"Would you say that you know the staff well?"

Hobday shrugged. "Pretty well. I interface with project managers, solutions architects, technical architects, service delivery managers, software designers, programmers, business analysts, software analysts, technical support, and accounts. I guess you could say that I know them well." He was doing his hardest to maintain his composure and control the conversation without being intimidated.

"Did you ever meet Linda Allen?" Scott asked. "She was in technical support."

Hobday cleared his throat. "The name rings a bell, but they have several people in technical support, so I can't put a face to the name."

Abby pulled out a picture of Linda Allen, taken from her

lounge, and presented it to him. It was a picture of her with Shannon to one side whilst she held baby Leo, when he was only a few months old.

Hobday maintained eye contact with Abby before lowering his gaze and focusing on the picture. His eyes didn't blink as he took in the image. He offered the slightest of nods.

"Mr Hobday? Do you recognise her?" Scott asked.

"Yes," was all he could offer.

"Yes, you recognise her? Yes, you've spoken to her? Yes, you've seen her?" Abby replied flippantly.

Hobday cleared his throat again. "Yes, I've seen her. And I spoke to her in passing. Just to offer a greeting or some nicety as we passed."

"Where were you last Sunday evening between six p.m. and midnight?"

Hobday shook his head, as if trying to shake his brain into recollecting his whereabouts on that night. "Off the top of my head, at home with the wife."

"Did you go out any point, even briefly?"

"What are you implying, Inspector?"

"Nothing. I need you to confirm your movements." Scott changed tack. "What do you do outside work?"

"I'm sorry? I'm not sure what that has to do with your investigation."

"Everything," Scott replied firmly. "Do you have a family?"

Hobday's eyes narrowed as they bore into Scott. "I'm married, but I don't have a family. We had a daughter, but she passed away a few days after being born prematurely." His gaze lowered to the desk and his shoulders dropped. He looked lost in deep thought.

"I'm sorry to hear that."

"Thank you," he muttered.

Scott continued. "Linda had two children. They have been taken into care temporarily until suitable next of kin are identified."

Hobday looked up at him. "Suitable, what does that mean?"

"Shannon, her daughter, will probably be cared for by Linda's mother, because the natural father is not best placed to look after her. And we're trying to trace Leo's father. Unfortunately, we have been unable to do that."

"I...I see. Do you mind me asking how she was murdered?"

"We can't go into detail, but she was raped, strangled...and suffocated." Scott studied Hobday's face for a few moments. He noticed the man's eyelids twitch, and a distinctive change in his complexion as the colour drained from him.

Scott and Abby stood. "Thank you for your time, Mr Hobday. We won't keep you any further. As the investigation proceeds, we may need to talk to you again."

Hobday saw them to the door, offering nothing more than a nod of his head.

"What did you make of that?" Abby asked, as they unwrapped their lunches in a sandwich bar in town. "He was uncomfortable throughout."

"He was hiding something, that's for sure. It was written on his face. He knows more than he's revealed so far, and he knows Linda better than he's letting on. I'm sure of that." Scott took a large chunk out of his tuna, mayo and sweetcorn sandwich. The change in Hobday's features and his eye movements had shown both guilt and sadness. If they were looking for the married man that Linda was involved with, Scott felt they might have just found him. For the moment though, he'd hold that theory and wait to see what else bubbled to the surface.

"Are you thinking what I'm thinking about Hobday and Linda?" Abby asked.

"Probably."

"So, what now?"

Scott wiped his mouth with a napkin. "More digging. We need to know more about Hobday's movements on that night, even if to do nothing more than eliminate him. Can you get on to that for me?"

Abby nodded, as she too tucked into her sandwich.

Scott tapped his forehead with the palm of his hand. "I still need to check in with David Levy, the councillor. I've not had much time to investigate the disappearance of his daughter since we spoke. The last thing I need is Levy running to CC Lennon."

"Good luck with that. Unless new information surfaces, she will be another statistic, unfortunately. But I guess he doesn't want to hear that. What parent does?"

Scott's phone vibrated in his pocket. He answered it to see Mike's name pop up on the screen. He listened for a few moments, nodding before raising a brow. "Interesting. We'll be back in fifteen minutes."

Abby pestered Scott after he hung up.

"Mike's been doing some digging around and come back with some good information. But even better than that, some new evidence has been presented that might be linked to our case."

"Really? What?" Abby asked, following Scott out of the door.

"A black-patent, high-heeled, peep-toe shoe."

25

Scott rushed through the station and made a beeline for his office, where Mike stood with arms crossed, staring at Scott's desk.

In two clear evidence bags were a black shoe and red underwear. Scott circled round and sat down, staring at the objects in silence. The shoe was clean. Light bounced off the black patent material. The other evidence bag had what appeared to be scrunched up red knickers. In contrast to the shoe, they were dirty and marked.

"Linked to Linda?" Abby suggested.

Mike shrugged. "It matches the items that were missing. And the shoebox we recovered from her house has a picture matching that shoe."

"And who brought it in?"

"A gentleman called Anil Shah and his wife, Minu. I suspect Mr Shah came to the station reluctantly, judging by his wife's mood."

"How did he come by them?" Scott asked, as he leant in to take a closer look.

"He's a keen cyclist. A road cyclist. He is one of those knobs who hogs the road and slows down the traffic." A hint of annoyance flashed in Mike's tone. "He's in one of the interview rooms downstairs. I thought you might want a word with him."

Scott nodded. "Get these bags to forensics immediately. Arrange for a buccal swab for our friend Mr Shah, although judging by the state of the knickers, I think we may have his DNA on it..."

Abby pulled a face in disgust and covered her mouth. "Men are such perverts," she fumed, and stepped out of the room.

"This case keeps turning up new stuff. I can't keep up with it," Scott said.

Mike nodded in agreement. "I was looking through the case files, and now we have a direct link between ours and the Cardiff case. What happens if there's more? We could pull a list from the system of more than a hundred women who are missing in the Sussex area, whether by choice or not." Mike pulled up a chair and dropped his heavy frame into it. "Some are taken out of the country; others disappear between the cracks and end up at the other end of the UK, not wanting to be found. What happens if our killer has struck before? There could be more bodies out there that we may never discover."

Scott understood Mike's concern. Some did meet an untimely death, and for the sake of their families, he always hoped officers could locate victims, to offer their families closure. But he was in no doubt that many were never found.

When he'd worked in Essex, Scott had heard many stories of how Epping Forest had been the final resting place for bodies over the last fifty years. The East End underworld was notorious for taking their victims in the dead of night and disposing of their bodies in the depths of the forest. Many were never found; either well buried or disposed of in such remote locations, it was unlikely that anyone would stumble upon them.

With Brighton surrounded by the Sussex Downs, it was possible and plausible that it, too, was the final resting place for many.

"It made me think," Mike continued. "Levy had asked you to look into the disappearance of his daughter, Rebecca. Whilst digging back through her case file, I picked up on the fact that Rebecca and Lexi Freeman were friends. And now Lexi is holed up with Dalca. There might be nothing in it; Brighton is a small enough place to know lots of people."

Scott sighed and ran his hands down his face. He blew out his cheeks. "I've got to pay David Levy a visit later, anyway. I feel bad I've done nothing much to investigate his case. But if we did that for everyone who asked us, there wouldn't be enough hours in the day. I've looked over the case file, and there's nothing more I would have done at the time, if I had been SIO."

Mike and Scott made their way down to the interview room and paused outside to exchange notes. "What have you got so far on Mr Shah?"

"Not a lot. I ran his name through the system. He's clean. To be honest, he looked like a rabbit caught in headlights. His wife was on his shoulder, just glaring at the back of his head. I tell you, if looks could kill, he'd be in the mortuary by now. She's one unhappy bunny. It was an effort controlling her. She was fuming about his porn addiction, fetishes, and the fact he's played away on at least one occasion."

"Judge, jury and executioner."

Mike rolled his eyes in agreement.

"A likely suspect?"

"I'm not sure, guv. You'll see when you go in. He's thin and spindly, around five-foot six. I can't imagine him strong enough to overpower Linda or Daisy. He may have an alter ego that comes out in certain situations, but judging by the way he is around his wife, I think he is a bit of a wimp. Linda wanted to be dominated. I think she would have eaten Shah for breakfast."

Anil Shah cut a desolate figure, as he sat with his arms close to his side and his hands firmly clenched on his lap. He looked like a naughty schoolboy waiting to be chastised by the head teacher.

His wife, Minu, sat to his side, her arms crossed, her lips pursed tight, and a cold, chilly stare that threatened to send an Arctic blast through the room. Despite her acidic appearance, Minu Shah was an attractive Asian female, with a blemish-free skin. She had a thin, pleasing face, framed by jet-black hair that cascaded over her shoulders.

Scott placed two evidence bags on the table, then went through the formalities and formal caution for the tape recorder. Shah stared at both nervously, not daring to look at his wife.

"Mr Shah, I'm Inspector Scott Baker, the Senior Investigating Officer on a murder investigation surrounding the death of a local woman. We believe these items may have belonged to the victim. I'd like you to begin by telling me how you came to be in possession of them."

Shah remained silent and stared at the table; embarrassment had robbed him of his voice.

Scott continued. "We launched a press appeal several days ago online and through local TV. You must have seen them?"

He offered the slightest of nods.

"Mr Shah, you're not doing yourself any favours here. You're being interviewed in connection with the rape and murder of Linda Allen. That's a serious matter. Do you understand?"

"Yes. I do."

"Of course, he does," Minu spat with venom. "I made him come here. My husband hung onto that stuff just to satisfy his own perverted curiosity. He makes me sick. He tosses off over stuff like this. Shoes, underwear, stockings, and porn mags. It's not the first time I found him doing this. He needs to be locked up,"

Scott held out a hand to calm Mrs Shah.

Mr Shah spoke with a soft voice. "I can't help myself."

Surges of excitement raced through Scott. Was this the man they'd been looking for? Could he be responsible for the deaths of Linda Allen and Daisy Callaghan?

"Where did you get these items from?" Scott asked, pointing at the evidence bags.

"From some filthy married woman, no doubt!" Minu shouted, as she took a swing at her husband.

Mike leant over the table and grabbed her arm in flight. She glared at him in return.

"Mrs Shah, if you continue to interrupt this interview, you will be removed," Mike said. "We are interested in what your husband has to say now, not you."

Minu sat back in her chair, a heavy scowl on her face, as she stared down the officers.

Scott returned his attention to Mr Shah, waiting for him to speak.

"I...I cycle every morning."

"Cycle? Is that what you call it?" Minu screamed. "I bet you just take your precious bike round to some tart, and –"

"Mrs Shah," Scott shouted. "If you carry on, I'll have you removed from this room. Do...I...Make...Myself...Clear?"

Scott's fiery glare extinguished the woman's wrath for the time being. She folded her arms across her chest and looked away in defiance.

Mr Shah continued without averting his gaze. "I've got a sixteen-mile circuit I follow. As I was coming back on my return leg, I saw what looked like a bag of rubbish in the middle of the road. I pulled over to the side, and because there were no cars on the road at that time of the morning, I went to have a look."

"Carry on," Scott said.

"Those things were in the bag. One shoe was wet and dirty, so I left it there. The other two things I just put in my rucksack and took them home with me."

"And what did you do with them when you took them home?"

Shah flushed with embarrassment and took a sip of water to quench his dry throat. "I get off playing with this stuff. My wife...and I aren't that adventurous."

Scott looked at Minu, who had placed a hand over her face. Tears trickled down her cheeks. "There's a big difference between adventurous and sick," she muttered.

"Were there any other items?" Scott asked.

Shah nodded. "Silver short skirt. But it was dirty, wet and muddy. I think cars must have driven over it a few times. The heel had broken off the other shoe."

Mike and Scott exchanged a glance. Shah had discovered the rest of Linda Allen's missing items.

Scott placed a small map on the table and asked Shah to identify the location. He'd arrange for officers to sweep the location immediately.

"Did you see anything else? Another vehicle parked close by, people walking, anything?"

Shah shook his head. "I did look around, but the place was deserted. I figured someone had thrown it away."

Mike interrupted, firmness in his voice. "Do you think a woman is going to go home without a skirt, underwear or shoes?"

Shah bowed his head, as he realised how pathetic he sounded.

Scott said, "No doubt you saw our press appeal, and we've had dozens of officers searching open land looking for these missing items, but you chose to ignore it. Even though you knew we desperately needed to find them? You were happy to withhold vital information from us?"

"Yes, Inspector."

"He would have kept them if I had not caught him," Minu interrupted. "I told him I wanted him out the house. I have put up with this for too long. He thought he could hide all this stuff from me. If our community finds out what he's like, the shame it would bring upon us is unimaginable. I was worried for my safety in case he *had* killed her."

"Did you know Linda Allen?" Scott asked Shah.

"No."

"Did you know Daisy Callaghan?"

Shah looked at Scott in puzzlement. "Who's that?"

"Another victim we believe has been killed by the same person." Scott thought about Linda's affair with a married man and baby Leo. Shah wasn't the man because of his ethnicity.

"I swear I don't know her."

"I'll ask you only once, have you been to Cardiff in the past twelve months?"

Shah held out his hands in defence. "No. I've never been there."

"Where were you on Sunday evening between six p.m. and midnight?"

Shah thought for a moment. "I met a colleague about six-thirty p.m., and we went for a drink."

"And where was that?"

"At the Stag pub."

The information piqued Scott's interest. The Stag pub was less than a hundred yards from The Greys Pub. Shah confirmed that he was there until around eight-thirty p.m., and after that made his way home. However, his wife contradicted him by saying that Shah hadn't returned until nearer eleven p.m. Shah said he took a long drive home but couldn't recall his exact route.

Scott laid out the bait. "You see, Mr Shah, I think you left the pub, and when you saw Linda Allen dressed in those heels –" Scott tapped the evidence bag, "– you followed her, attacked her, raped her and then dumped her body. And to further your self-gratification, took these items as souvenirs."

Shah slammed his hands on the table. "No. I don't know who she is. I just found those things. I haven't killed anyone."

"We'll see about that. In the meantime, you are facing a

charge of withholding vital information in connection with the rape and murder of Linda Allen. We will also take a saliva sample from you and seize your car for forensic analysis."

Shah bowed his head. His wife sobbed.

26

Scott left the team to progress enquiries on Anil Shah. Scott's instincts told him that this wasn't their man, but they needed to cover every base. Abby stayed behind to oversee the process. She would arrange for swabs to be taken, and Shah's car to be impounded and taken to the station on a low-loader for examination. She instructed Mike and Raj to follow up on Shah's movements last Sunday and identify if he had been to Cardiff in the past twelve months.

Scott arrived at David Levy's house. It was a small, terraced property in the heart of Brighton. By the way Levy spoke and had conducted himself, Scott had visions of him living in a large, detached house. He had a presence and air of authority. Having investigated Levy's background, it transpired to Scott that his character traits had been shaped by his time in the RAF, followed by several management positions in local businesses.

Levy answered the door not long after Scott had rung the bell. He greeted Scott with a firm handshake and the smallest of smiles. Pain sat heavy on the man's shoulders as he led Scott through to the lounge. It was a small room, with the traditional three-piece-suite sofa and two armchairs either side taking central position in the room. A large TV hung above the fireplace. Scott's eyes were drawn to the array of family portraits and photographs that crammed the ledge.

"Thank you for coming, Inspector," Levy said. "I thought you had forgotten about our conversation..."

Scott nearly had but would never have admitted it. He wondered whether Levy's last statement was just that, a statement of resignation or a question.

"Yes, I'm sorry for not getting back to you sooner. But as you can imagine with our ongoing murder investigation, we've had our hands full."

"Yes, of course. Of course. A dreadful situation. And I understand that resources have to be prioritised." Levy sounded almost apologetic. His gaze dropped to the floor.

"How have you been holding up since we last spoke?"

"Same as before. Every time the doorbell rings...I know I'm being foolish, but I expect it to be Becky. I imagine her rushing through the door, and me throwing my arms around her."

"It's not foolish at all. I imagine every parent in your situation would feel the same." Scott felt his pain. Losing a child was difficult for any parent, but losing a child and not knowing what happened to them must be a living nightmare.

"Have you any news?" Levy asked.

Scott needed to bend the truth. "My team have reopened her file, and we've been going over all the statements, checking and double-checking them. We are reviewing information relating to the last sightings of Rebecca." Scott hated that word reviewing. It was vague and abstract and could mean anything, from a mere glance to a deep dive.

Levy nodded. He looked at the mantelpiece where memories of happier times had been captured in an array of silver, gold and wooden picture frames. Scott followed Levy's eyes.

"She looked happy in them," Scott said.

Levy nodded again. "She was...She is." Referring to her in the past appeared to send a thunderbolt of pain through his chest. "She always had a smile, and her laugh would reach every corner of the house. Just looking at her would fill me with so much pride and joy. She could raise a smile in me without saying a word." He pursed his lips; the slightest of chin wobbles indicated how hard he was fighting to keep it together.

"Mr Levy, I'd like to ask you a few questions, if that's okay?"

The man shrugged. "Of course."

"The circumstances around your daughter's disappearance are puzzling and out of character for her. Linda Allen, I'm curious whether that name rings a bell with you. Had Rebecca ever mentioned her name?"

Levy narrowed his eyes at Scott, as if trying to second-guess his motive for asking the question. "Other than recent reports, I'm afraid not. Not that I can remember."

"How about the name Lexi Freeman? Does that sound familiar?"

Levy's brow lifted in recognition. "I remember Becky saying she had hung out with her a few times in local pubs and clubs. I don't think they were tight as friends, more like social friends I guess, but her name cropped up occasionally.

Personally, I wasn't too keen on her. She called around here once looking for Becky. I was immediately turned off by her hard exterior. She was abrupt and agitated. Is she a person of interest?"

"Not directly. But she is living with Linda Allen's ex-boyfriend. It's a complicated web, but there are tenuous links between Rebecca, Linda Allen, and Lexi Freeman that I believe are worth looking into."

Levy stiffened up and straightened his back, as he listened to Scott.

Scott continued. "So, I'm wondering if Rebecca had mentioned any names to you, even if in passing, that you can recall now."

Levy looked off into the distance, as if deep in thought. He chased back through his memories. He shook his head. "I'm sure she mentioned many names, including the Freeman woman. She was forever going out, and it was tough keeping up with who she was going out with, where she was headed, or who she was meeting. One name seemed to blend into another."

"I know you produced a witness statement regarding her disappearance, and I've read it. But would you mind recalling those events for me now?"

Levy nodded wearily. "We had breakfast as normal. She pottered about in her room for a while, like she did most mornings, sorting out her hair and makeup before deciding what to do. Women do that, don't they?"

Scott remained silent, not wishing to disrupt Levy's train of thought.

"She breezed downstairs and shouted from the bottom step that she was going out for a while. I managed to come out of the study in time to catch her before she left. I asked her normal things like whether she had anything planned and how long she'd be gone. Becky replied that she was going shopping for a new outfit and some underwear, which made me blush a tad. She promised she wouldn't be long because she had a *hot* date that evening..."

"That was the last time you saw her?"

Levy nodded.

"Was there anything different in her mood or her behaviour that day?"

"No. Nothing."

"You mentioned in your statement that you phoned around, trying to find out what happened to her when she didn't return home?"

Levy frowned. "Hmm. I phoned a few of her friends, but no one had spoken to her that day. As you know from the witness statements, she was seen in town, but disappeared off the face of the earth."

"Looking at her case file, the investigating team could not come up with a person of interest or suspect."

"I know, Inspector. But something tells me that more could have been done. I know people disappear all the time, but in broad daylight, in the middle of the day? In a busy town centre? Surrounded by people and CCTV?" Frustration tinged his barrage of questions.

"I appreciate that. Officers spent hours trawling through CCTV footage taken in the town centre. They looked at recordings from taxi ranks, the bus terminus and the train station, without luck. Despite a press appeal, there were no sightings of her. I can't go into detail, but I can assure you, having reviewed the file, that extensive resources were deployed to locate her."

There was that word again, review.

Scott pressed. "Do you have your own theory regarding her disappearance?"

Levy shifted in his seat and looked at Scott, with determination in his eyes. "Becky changed in the last few months before she disappeared."

"In what way?"

"I can't quite put my finger on it, but she became distant and aloof. Not in a horrible kind of way. She was still the same fun Becky, but something had changed, whether that was part of the growing up process or something going on in her life, I don't know."

"Did she appear upset over anything?"

"Not as far as I know. Becky was going out just as much, but she would say less about where she was going, and who she was hanging around with. It was about the same time that that Freeman woman came on the scene. Whether she is connected or not, I'm not sure. But something about that woman bothered me. I guess it was me being the protective dad and not wanting my daughter to mix with people who might be a bad influence on her."

Levy fell silent for a few moments, then added, "Who am I kidding? How many parents really know what their kids get up to?"

A complex web of relationships formed in Scott's mind. He had referred to a tenuous link earlier in the conversation, and it was nothing more than that. Nevertheless, it bothered him.

"Do you think the Freeman woman is connected in some way?" Levy asked.

"I can't be certain," Scott offered. "At this stage, I have a murder investigation and Rebecca's disappearance, and Lexi Freeman's name appears connected to both."

Levy shuffled forward and perched on the edge of his chair. "But you should talk to her? And if you don't, then I will. As a family we still need answers."

Scott tried to placate the man. "We will be, Mr Levy, I can assure you of that. And as soon as we have, if what she has to say has any relevance to Rebecca's disappearance, then I will inform you."

27

His visits to her were nothing more than a chore. His hopes for her had faded not long after he'd befriended her and brought her here. Frustration gnawed away at him. Anger simmered inside him at the thought of the wasted hours and risks he'd taken.

He'd made his mind up. She was nothing more than a liability.

Heavy, slippery, and wet, he slid the grate away from the entrance to the inspection chamber and peered into the dark hole that disappeared into the earth. He glanced around to ensure he was alone before he flicked on the torch and descended into the blackness, taking each slippery rung of the metal ladder slow and steady.

"Wake up, you silly bitch. I've brought you something to eat and drink – not that you need it, or deserve it."

Silence was his only answer.

"Did you not fucking hear me? Don't piss me off."

He paused a few metres above the metal inspection platform and looped one arm around a rung, whilst he shone his torch into the darkness below.

A wave of panic coursed through his veins when he saw nothing but the bedding she had lain upon.

"Fuck..."

He swept the light from his torch in left to right arcs as he searched for her. He then followed the trail of the cable. His eyes widened, his breath became ragged and harsh, as he navigated the final few steps as fast as he could.

Just her head remained visible, the cable still attached around her neck. He peered over the edge of the small, crescent-shaped metal platform and saw the rest of her body dangling. Her feet hovered just inches from the floor of the chamber.

He had misjudged the length of the cable. He thought he had added enough slack in case she fell over the edge. Emma was dead, eyes fixated, vacant.

She was gone.

Cold and pale.

Rats scuttled to safety as the beam of light trapped them in mid-frenzy, gnawing away at her feet. He watched their black, beady eyes, sleek brown fur, with teeth like steel pincers, as they scrabbled, scurried, and climbed to evade the glare. A frantic brown wave. A seething, living, furry tsunami of terrified animals. The sight sent a shiver down his spine.

"You've done me a favour, you fucking moron. You were nothing but a big tease. I hope it fucking hurt."

He thumped the side of his head with the torch a few times. He hadn't thought this through. With them being so far down, it would be impractical to heave her body back up to the surface. He knew from experience how hard it was to shift a dead body. The last thing he wanted was to be caught with a stiff in the boot of his car. He removed the keys from his rucksack and unlocked the padlock that secured the cable in place.

Her body crumpled to the ground below, giving a soft thud as it landed. Dinner had arrived early for the rodents. More rats squeezed through crevices and joined in the feast.

28

The mornings were a lot colder and darker since the tentacles of winter had taken hold. Scott loved his early morning runs along the seafront during the early part of the year. With the onset of winter, and the cold and biting wind that whipped in off the sea, his runs were bracing, hard and tiring.

He'd left Cara in bed. Rather than be tempted by her promises and pleas to remain, he had crept out of the house before six a.m.

Scott stopped halfway between Palace Pier and the marina to catch his breath. Not that he was unfit, but he liked to stop and just stare out to sea. He found it therapeutic and mesmerising. He would allow his mind to drift and his eyes to scan the horizon. It was one of those rare occasions where he could switch off and think of nothing. An opportunity to declutter his mind.

He narrowed his eyes, spotting the faint outline of a cargo ship on the horizon. From this distance it appeared static. He wondered where it had set sail from, and its destination. He imagined life at sea to be a solitary one, floating across hundreds, if not thousands square miles of ocean.

The waves rolled in beneath him, each of them as strong and bold as the last. They looked like a fifties hairdo, over-pronounced in the crown and mesmerising, making it impossible to avert his gaze. As they hit, they brought with them the music of the beach, the percussion section roaring from the stony bed below, yet softened by the water. Magical, relaxing and pleasurable. It was like listening to his own relaxation CD of ocean sounds.

Life was good, better than it had been in a long time, and for that he was truly grateful. The darkness that had been his constant companion for many years drifted away, much in the same way as the cargo ship. His relationship with Cara had blossomed into something he hadn't expected to find. His friendship with Abby was rock solid. If he was honest, he would be lost without both women in his life.

He inhaled a large, lungful of salty air and allowed it to permeate every cell of his being before finishing his run. He needed to get back and tell Cara how much he loved her.

WHILST MOST PEOPLE enjoyed lazy Sunday mornings, where a family breakfast or Sunday morning walk provided the order of the day, followed by the preparation of and indulgence in an afternoon roast, Scott and the team were hard at work.

The team gathered around the incident board. Scott sensed a general feeling of laziness and boredom amongst the team. Whether it was because it was Sunday or the case was getting to them, he was unsure.

It was a common problem that most officers faced. Crime never stood still. Robbery, rape, assaults, and murder were committed daily. And the saying 'today's news is tomorrow's fish and chip paper' held true. The longer an investigation continued, the less the chance of success, and this challenge played on Scott's mind.

Scott focused on the small successes they'd had rather than the many questions still unanswered. The results of the DNA analysis had helped but the suspect was still unclear, and therefore remained the primary driver for their investigations.

They had sent the swab taken from Shah to forensics, along with samples from Richards and Dalca, both of whom had been reluctant to submit samples to begin with. A minor delay at the forensics lab meant that Dalca's buccal swab hadn't been frozen immediately. The sample had degraded in quality which had deemed the result inconclusive. Scott had issued a new request for a sample from Dalca, and Raj and Helen had visited Dalca to get it, much to Dalca's amusement.

Richards, on the other hand had refused to provide any DNA sample from a mouth swab or head hair root, or skin sample from his hands and arms. Ignoring the man's non-compliance and knowing that they didn't need his permission to do this, Raj headed to the bathroom to retrieve Richards's toothbrush, whilst Helen made a beeline for the bedroom to retrieve a hair sample from the pillows.

Helen had commented that they had almost called for backup after Richards became abusive. His alcohol-fuelled bravado had caused a tense stand-off.

Scott said, "Helen, I want you to have a chat with Jackie Cartwright, and then Claire Allen. Both have had time to consider the situation, and I'm convinced that one of them, if not both have more to tell us."

"Do you think they're hiding something?"

"I think her mother is. There is something about her I can't quite put my finger on. Both Shannon and Leo are her grandchildren, but she only talked about Shannon, and looking after her. She hardly mentioned Leo, and her whole persona changed when his name came up."

"And Jackie?"

Scott shrugged a shoulder. "I want you to go through her statement again. See if any fresh insights popup."

Helen nodded.

Scott turned towards the incident board where pictures of Linda Allen and Daisy Callaghan stared out across the CID floor. "We know he's killed before. My concern is whether Councillor Levy's daughter may have been another victim. Ordinarily, we could treat her as another missing person. Lexi Freeman knew her, and now Lexi is Dalca's girlfriend. That makes me think Rebecca Levy may have come to harm. Without a body I can't prove it, but it's something we need to consider."

"Should we pay her a visit today, guv?" Abby suggested. "Nothing better than being disturbed by the police on a Sunday morning."

The comment was met with ripples of laughter.

Scott said, "Whoever Linda met at the pub has to be our suspect. He was the last person to see her alive. Dalca said he was with Lexi on that night, and we saw the phone footage that confirmed they had sex. Richards hasn't given us a decent alibi other than watching TV. Linda and Richards weren't the best of friends, so I can't imagine she was meeting him in the pub. But I think it's worth leaning on him."

"So, we're back to a mystery man, or married mystery man, or both?" Mike muttered.

The team fell silent as they weighed up their options.

Scott said, "Mike, bring Richards in for a chat. He's shown violence towards Linda in the past, and the pair didn't see eye to eye. Don't forget he found her in bed with someone, and she was seeing other guys, so the motives of jealousy and revenge are worth exploring with him. He'll moan about police harassment, but don't take any of his shit. He likes us as much as we like him. Rattle his cage and keep a close eye on him to see what he does."

29

Richards looked anything but pleased as he sat in the interview room. His arms were crossed tightly across his chest as he slouched in the chair. Anger boiled as hot as lava. It churned within, hungry for destruction, and he knew it would spew forth in a massive eruption before he could stop it. The pressure from this raging sea of anger would make him say things he did not mean, or express thoughts he'd suppressed for weeks.

The room was every shade of grey, from washed-out concrete to steel blue. Every line was straight, every corner sharp, and the chairs felt as comfortable as a train station bench. He hated the place. They had left him sitting here for twenty minutes, whilst the uniformed officer by the door stood and observed him. Richards shot the officer menacing looks; he hated *them* as much as he hated this place.

It was never good news when the police came knocking at his door. The neighbours had expressed their disgust as they'd peered through the cracks in their front doors. It pissed him off to be woken on a Sunday. A late-night of watching shit on TV had been made bearable by three quarters of a bottle of rum. It had left him groggy, with a parched throat and malaise.

Mike sauntered in and nodded at the uniformed officer before giving Richards the biggest grin he could muster. Raj followed behind, doing likewise. They had both agreed to wind Richards up from the outset.

"Sorry to keep you waiting, Mr Richards. My colleague and I were just finishing a late Sunday breakfast," Mike announced, as he flopped in the chair opposite and rubbed his full stomach. He made a point of looking at Raj.

Richards sneered in disdain at Mike.

"I understand you've declined the offer of a duty solicitor?" Mike said.

"I've got nothing to fucking hide. The sooner you clowns get on with this, the sooner I can leave this shithole."

"Don't be so keen, Mr Richards," Raj goaded. "With the way things are going, you might end up spending more of your time here. We're very hospitable, with luxurious accommodations, don't you think?"

Mike loaded up the tape recorder.

"I'm stuffed," he said, turning to Raj. "I knew I shouldn't have had that third sausage and those extra bits of bacon. Two sausages, four rashers of bacon, two fried eggs, beans and mushrooms, and lashings of hot tea was more than enough. Eyes bigger than my belly." He laughed.

Raj turned to Richards. "Have you had breakfast?"

"No and I wouldn't mind what you just had."

"I'm sorry, Mr Richards. The station canteen is only for officers and prisoners. And you're neither."

Richards's frustration grew. "What did you drag me in here for, anyway?"

Mike said, "As you know, Mr Richards, we're investigating the rape and murder of your ex-wife Linda Allen. We would like to ask you a few more questions."

"I've told you everything already. You're wasting my time."

As Mike leant across the table, his face took on a serious edge. "This is the mother of your child. Someone set out to rape, strangle, and murder Linda Allen. We are trying to find out who committed this atrocious act. Someone left her body half-naked and partially buried. Their heinous crime has left two children without a mother. I don't see that as wasting anyone's time. Do you?"

Richards smirked. "Ten out of ten for effect."

Mike continued. "You mentioned that Linda had been seeing other men. In fact, you came home once to discover her in bed with someone."

"So?"

"It's rather convenient that you returned home on the same night she brought someone home. Do you not think?"

"No."

"From your interview with my colleagues, you stayed out a lot. You see, I find it too much of a coincidence that Linda had never brought someone back before, as far as you are aware. But on that night, when she finally did bring someone to your marital home, you decided to return? How damn convenient for you."

"It's was my home. I was free to come and go as I wanted."

Mike said, "How did you feel about Linda after witnessing her blatant betrayal?"

Richards shrugged his shoulders. "I felt nothing. Not for her anyway. She was a whore. Yeah, it pissed me off. But more about the fact that a man, another man, was in my house. I couldn't give a toss if she was in someone else's bed. But to do that under my roof? She crossed the line."

Mike gave Raj a sideways glance.

He continued. "Had she crossed the line enough to be raped, strangled and murdered?"

"Like I told the others and I'm telling you, you ain't going to fucking pin anything on me. You know and I know that she got slapped by me on more than one occasion. Yeah, she crossed the line. But I wouldn't cross the line and go as far as kill someone."

Mike pushed harder. "But she pissed you off. She fucked another man in *your* bed. She took a big risk knowing you could come home at any moment. But it appears that the thrill and prospect of sharing a night of passion with someone else far outweighed any fear she had about being discovered by you."

Every time Mike opened his mouth, Richards got angrier. All that rage spewed forth faster than lava. He launched across the table and tried to grab Mike by his tie. Mike's meaty hand swept in an arc and came down on Richards's arm, pinning it to the table. The uniformed officer raced from his post by the door and pulled Richards back in his chair.

Unfazed by the outburst, Mike continued. "That temper of yours, it's a bit twitchy. It doesn't take much for you to lose it, does it? Is that how you felt when you had time to think about what Linda had done to you?"

Richards barked at the officers, spittle flying from his mouth in all directions, "I didn't fucking kill her, but good fucking riddance to the bitch!"

Richards claimed he would press charges for police

harassment. His idle threats faded fast when Mike suggested that a counterclaim of an attempted assault on a police officer would have him dragged back in quicker than his feet could touch the floor.

"Listen, I want you off my back," Richards said. "Unless you've got evidence to link me to your case, stay the fuck away from me. As I said, you've got the wrong man. Speak to your boss. Like I told him when he came to see me, you are barking up the wrong tree."

Mike gritted his teeth, his jaw flexing. "I don't care what tree we are barking up. If you are implicated in this, I will find that evidence, and you'll spend a lot more time inside a small room with grey walls."

The inference wasn't lost on Richards. He stared at the table for a few moments, rolling his thumbs in a circle, knowing that what he knew would get them off his back. "The married fella she was having an affair with. He's Leo's dad."

Mike looked up from his notes. "Go on. But if you're doing this to pull my chain, you'll have to try harder."

"As God is my witness," Richards replied, looking up at the ceiling. "Hobday. That's who she was banging."

DALCA LIVED in a small property towards the back of town in a less-than-desirable location. His apartment was one of four in a converted Victorian house, with crumbling cream paint on the outside, and a red wooden door that was faded due to years of sunlight.

When Scott noticed the door was on the latch, he pushed it open. He entered a small hallway with an apartment to his left and right, and another two upstairs. Dalca lived upstairs.

Abby didn't hold the handrail. Her OCD kicked in, and she wrinkled her nose at the thought of the hundreds of grimy hands that had gripped the banister before her. Judging from the environment, she doubted if many of those hands had been clean.

Scott hammered on Dalca's door and heard footsteps on the other side. He imagined whoever stood behind it was peering through the small spyhole right now, deciding whether to open the door.

"Who is it?" came a male voice. Scott recognised Dalca's thick European accent.

Scott raised a brow at his question. They had questioned Dalca only a few days ago. "It's the police, so stop pissing about. If you want me to shout louder so your neighbours hear, then keep hiding behind that door."

Scott heard the key turning the lock. The door opened and Dalca peered around the corner. "What you want?"

"It's not you we want. We need a word with your girlfriend, Lexi Freeman."

"She's...she's in bed."

"I don't care if she's fast asleep, we need to talk to her, now," Abby said, passing Scott. She pushed Dalca to one side as he remonstrated.

Abby led the way, peering in each doorway off the main corridor before she found the main bedroom at the back of the apartment. Lexi Freeman was sitting up in bed. Her fiery, red hair tumbled down her shoulders. She had a dainty chin, and a pair of dark-brown eyes peeked out from under her fringe. She glanced up at them, blowing out smoke circles. She tapped her cigarette in the ashtray.

"Lexi Freeman?" Abby asked.

"Might be," she replied.

Abby and Scott held up their warrant cards. "I'm Detective Sergeant Trent, and this is Detective Inspector Baker. We'd like to ask you a few questions."

The woman shrugged nonchalantly and looked out the window.

Dalca stood behind the officers, tight-lipped, dressed in nothing more than a T-shirt and boxer shorts.

"We are investigating the rape and murder of Linda Allen," Abby continued.

"Well, then you need to speak to Andrei, not me."

"It's not Dalca that we're here to question. We're trying to build a better picture of Linda's background. You know her ex-husband John Richards, right?"

"Who doesn't?" Her reply was abrupt and uninterested.

"What can you tell me about him?"

She turned to face Abby. "I know as much as you. In fact, you probably know more. He's an aggressive bastard, especially when he's had a few drinks. He doesn't care for anyone else but himself. Give him a four-pack, or a bottle of rum, and he's as happy as Larry."

"And did you hear anything else about him?"

Lexi looked puzzled.

"Anything about how he was towards women? We know about his temper. Do you think he would go further than that?"

Lexi's eyes widened. "Murder? Are you asking me whether he was capable of murder? Linda?"

"You tell me?" Abby replied.

Lexi paused for a moment, thinking things through, deciding what to say. "Andrei once mentioned that Linda feared Richards and his violence. Linda said it worried her that one day he was going to do her permanent damage. He laid into her on the night he found her in bed with someone else. He tried to force himself on her."

"He tried to rape her?" Scott asked.

Lexi twisted her mouth. "Sounded like it. But that's all I'm going to say. I don't want to get involved, right?"

Scott turned to leave, but then stopped. "By the way, how's Rebecca Levy these days?" He asked in a matter-of-fact way, as if in passing conversation, to gauge her reaction.

The question had shocked Lexi, because her mouth dropped and her eyes widened. "Rebecca? But she's been missing for years. How would I know?"

"No reason, but I wondered if you'd heard from her? Her parents still hope that one day she'll be found. I can't imagine the pain they must be going through every day."

Lexi grimaced. "Why do you expect me to know anything about it? She could be dead..." She trailed off.

"Because we're reviewing the case again and looking for anything that might help us find out what happened to her. So perhaps you heard something...or saw something that day she disappeared. I understand you were close friends. Shared the same social circle?"

Lexi dropped her head and wound a tissue around her finger. "She was my bestie. Yeah, it hurt when she disappeared. She was sad with life, hated being at home sometimes. We often spoke of heading to Greece to work in a bar and just chill, if you know what I mean. But it never happened. One minute she was here, next she was gone."

"Would she have gone to Greece without you?"

"No way."

30

Mike had put in a call to Scott not long after his interview with Richards. The recent discoveries they both had to share made for an interesting conversation. Upon hearing Scott's news, Mike had offered nothing more than a derogatory comment about Hobday having his cake and eating it too. Mike had dropped another bombshell regarding Hobday, which interested Scott further.

Hearing about Richards' behaviour in the interview did nothing more than confirm Scott's suspicions about the man. His violent tendencies still made him the key suspect.

Scott called Hobday, informed him he needed to speak to him as a matter of urgency. Hobday insisted that it could wait for Monday morning as he didn't appreciate the intrusion on his home life. When Scott told him the reason for the call, Hobday agreed to meet them at the station.

Scott and Abby made their way to the interview room to find Hobday pacing the room, looking less than relaxed. He was unshaven, and wearing a crumpled T-shirt and faded jeans. Deep worry lines creased his forehead. He looked nothing like the professional they had met the last time.

Scott thanked Hobday for sparing the time. He did the formal introductions for the benefit of the tape and provided the necessary caution. Hobday refused the offer of having a solicitor present, citing it as an overreaction, as he had nothing to hide.

"We wanted to talk to you about Linda Allen," Scott said. "After further enquiries, we understand now you knew her better than you suggested during our last discussion."

Hobday said nothing.

"Mr Hobday. Let me ask you again. Where were you on Sunday evening between six p.m. and midnight?"

"As I said before, I was at home with my wife."

"All evening?"

"Yes."

"And you are a hundred percent certain you didn't go out at all that evening in your car?"

"Yessss," he replied, impatiently.

"You see, Mr Hobday, I've just been informed by one of my officers, that following an extensive search of CCTV footage, your car was picked up on an ANPR camera that night less than a mile from where Linda's body was found."

Hobday's face drained of colour. His features sagged. "It must be a mistake."

"Are you suggesting that someone else was driving your car?"

"No. I didn't go out."

Scott slid the image still across the table to Hobday. It was a picture of him behind the wheel, captured by a camera.

Hobday swallowed and glanced at the two officers. Scott let the power of silence build in the room.

"You can see our predicament now, can't you, Mr Hobday?" Scott said. "You were near where Linda's body was found. And yet, when we first asked you, you were anything but truthful, citing that you had been at home all evening with your wife. My question is what would make you lie?"

Incoherent mutterings slipped from Hobday's lips.

"So, Mr Hobday, rather than dig yourself into an even bigger hole, why don't we start from the beginning. Where were you on Sunday night between six p.m. and midnight?"

Hobday interlaced his fingers and put his elbows on the table. He rested his chin on his hands. "I'd gone to see Linda. But when I got to her house, her car wasn't there. After that, I went back home."

"You know her better than you claimed to when we first spoke?"

Hobday chewed his lip and shifted nervously in his seat. The man nodded, as his gaze darted around the room a moment. Then his shoulders dropped in resignation. "I did. We initially made contact through a dating website. We exchanged messages like you do, and then..."

"Go on, Mr Hobday."

"We saw each other, just casual encounters to start with. A hotel room here and there. Then she wanted to make it racier. We would drive out of town into the woods and have sex outdoors. She was voracious. She always wanted sex, and the more daring it was, the more it turned her on."

"And she was married at the time?" Scott knew the answer already.

He nodded. "I was adamant to keep this as discreet as possible. Especially because I'm..."

"Married?"

Hobday's face flushed tomato red.

"Was it a sex game that went wrong?" Scott asked. "She wanted it rough. We know that she was into erotic asphyxiation. Did it go too far?"

"No. No. You have it all wrong. I didn't kill her."

"How do we have it all wrong, Mr Hobday? Would you care to elaborate?"

"We got on well. She was so easy to get on with. Don't get me wrong. I love my wife. We have a great relationship and a half-decent, sexual relationship. But it faded away after we lost our child. Something inside my wife changed. She kept longing for another baby but she had gone off the idea of sex. It was my wife's idea."

Scott and Abby shot each other a perplexed look.

"What was her idea?" Abby asked.

"Me having sex outside my marriage. My wife knew she couldn't give me what I wanted and she felt guilty. She said if I loved her and would never leave her, she would turn a blind eye if I had sex elsewhere. There was only one condition attached."

"And that was?"

"That I came home to her every evening, and I would love no other. Then Linda fell pregnant. It wasn't planned. We took precautions. But on one occasion, it wasn't enough."

"Leo?" Scott asked.

Hobday nodded. "I said I would pay for a termination. With a child of her own, I thought she would have agreed. But as the pregnancy continued, something changed. She wanted to keep the baby."

"And you didn't?"

Hobday shook his head. "No. It was the last thing I wanted. Well, yes and no. We argued a few times over it. But she wouldn't budge."

"Were you angry?"

"A bit. But not in the way you are thinking. I was shocked more than anything else. I suggested that my wife and I could adopt her baby, especially after what my wife had been through. We could give the baby a better life than Linda could. Though, I'm not sure my wife would have agreed. I said it in the heat of the moment. Linda pleaded with me to let her keep the baby. She said she wanted nothing from me. But I felt responsible and agreed to help financially."

Scott said, "We checked her bank records, and there are no substantial deposits in her bank account."

"There wouldn't be. She wanted cash instead. She said her day-to-day expenses, the cot, nappies and such were what she needed help with. I would drop off an envelope each month, which had a few hundred pounds in it."

"If you are Leo's closest living relative, then you would have legal rights over the child?"

"Yes."

"Did you kill Linda in order to get the baby?"

"No!"

SCOTT READ the first of the DNA results he was expecting. He leant back in his chair and cursed under his breath. The semen sample taken from Linda Allen was a negative match for Anil Shah. He was out of the frame. That news flooded

Scott with a mixture of emotions. Anger that the results had come back negative, but also relief that he could cross at least one suspect off his list.

31

He'd been looking forward to this all day. She had agreed to meet him. With the last one out of the way, he could focus on Katrina. This one sounded up for it. Their messages had become dirtier as the days had passed. The photographs had become racier. She looked like a better proposition than Emma, whose body lay in the bottom of the darkened pit, offering a handsome reward to the hungry critters that called that shithole their home.

He agreed to meet her in a pub, the same way he had done with the others. There were several pubs he preferred, chosen for their locations. Away from busy main roads, CCTV footage, and road traffic. All things that could trip him up.

He sat outside, waiting and watching punters come and go from the pub. There weren't as many on a Sunday night. He had seen her saunter up the street, dressed in ever-so-tight jeans that clung to her legs. He imagined her hot and sweaty crotch. She wore black-patent high heels, something he had insisted upon. Her black leather jacket was wrapped tightly around her, shielding her from the cold air.

Fifteen minutes. He liked to keep them waiting. His phone had bleeped three times already. Messages from her, asking where he was. He gave her a lame excuse about taking a wrong turn. It bought him some time.

He walked in, hood up, and muttered a few words to her about how he had somewhere better to go that she would love. She followed him out. He had been in the pub for no more than sixty seconds. Not enough time for anyone to recall his face or recognise his clothing.

She appeared excited at first as he told her about a remote pub which hosted a local band on a Sunday night. A pub where he knew a bartender who would ensure free drinks all night. That promise alone had sealed the deal for her.

They didn't go to the pub, stopping instead in a lay-by to kiss, exploring each other's mouths. She thrust her hand down his jeans searching out his cock, as he groped her breasts.

Wanting to take it further, he suggested that they disappear into the woods for no more than a few moments. At first, she was reluctant to venture out in the darkness, preferring the warmth of the car. She relented after he persisted.

Only a few yards into the darkened forest, he spun on his heels and punched her in the face. The blow sent her sprawling backwards to the sodden earth. With her mind dazed, and her face erupting in pain, he set upon her. He rained down one furious blow after another on her. Using his knees to pin her arms to her sides, he straddled her. He could feel moisture on his knuckles from her blood, blood that was trickling from her nose and her burst top lip.

She made little sound. Slightly dazed but conscious, she writhed on the ground, desperate to slip free. Her legs kicked wildly, catching on fallen branches and decaying leaf matter. Her precious, black patent heels soon became smothered in dirty, wet mud.

Katrina put up a valiant fight. In his twisted mind, it was a play fight. She said she liked it rough. All women liked it rough. She had told him so. Her fantasy was being kidnapped and held down, whilst at the mercy of men who raped and abused her body. *This is what she wanted, and I'm just the man to give it to her.*

With one hand, and most of his body weight leaning on her throat, he reached into his back pocket and pulled out a clear plastic bag. The harder he sat down on her chest, the more it pushed the air from her lungs. Small, thin and petite, she continued to struggle.

With his free hand, he pulled the bag over her head. Her head tossed from side to side, desperate to escape the cocoon. He removed his hand from her throat and reached inside his jacket to pull out the duct tape. Wrapping it around her neck several times, the tape entombed her face inside a plastic trap that inflated and deflated with each breath she took. He grabbed her arms next, binding her hands and wrists together in the same position a person would be when they were praying. But prayers would not help her today.

Desperate to experience her, he grabbed at her jeans and pulled them down. She wasn't wearing any underwear – again at his insistence. Whilst she clawed at the plastic, he thrust his hardened member into her.

His body twitched, his heartbeat quickened. His breath came in shallow gasps as he drove into her, each thrust accompanied by a grunt. His body shuddered as he climaxed. He collapsed on top of her exhausted, the weight of his body crushing and causing her to gasp.

As the seconds passed, her head thrashed less frequently. The bag inflated less and less, before it stilled. The fight gone from her as her life slipped away.

He had chosen this spot, as it was only a short distance to carry her to the inspection chamber.

Having no further need for her, he pulled back the grate, and rolled her crumpled body over the edge and into the hole. A few seconds later there was a dull thud, as her body hit the shaft floor.

He shone his torch into the darkened space.

Dinner for the inhabitants.

32

Scott spent most of the night tossing and turning, unable to sleep, his mind whirring like a complex timepiece. One thought locked into another, and then another, with no real clarity.

Despite learning more about baby Leo's parentage and uncovering the identity of the married man involved in an affair with Linda, there were still too many uncertainties. As he stared up at the darkened ceiling, his thoughts turned to Linda and the web of complexity she had weaved into her life. Single parents up and down the country had a tough time of it on the best of days. Childcare, tight budgets, stressful jobs, plus the emotional and mental well-being of their own children, left little time for themselves. Every day was a challenge for them. Any social life was a luxury.

To weave in a complicated love life comprising of sexual relations with more than one man confounded Scott further. Linda was a complex character. Hard-working, determined, fun, and yet she'd been clever, forceful, passionate, perhaps even desperate. Her ads had been nothing more than explicit pleas. Attempts to spice up her life, satisfy her sexual desires, and feel wanted. The men she'd been in contact with had wanted her, but one person had taken it too far.

Despite the best efforts of the high-tech team to glean data from her phone, much of the history had been deleted. It was anyone's guess as to how much evidence had been lost. Scott knew they would never know the extent of the network she had been in contact with. A lucky break for the sadistic killer, a missed opportunity for the investigating team.

CARA HAD SENSED the turmoil in Scott's mind as he drove her to the mortuary in silence. She tried to keep the conversation going. Scott offered nothing more than one-word answers, a "yes" here, "no" there, and "perhaps" were as much as she could squeeze from him. Regardless, his terse replies didn't upset or annoy her. She understood and sympathised with the difficulties he faced. He would often come home, unable to switch off. She could see his mind drift as they watched TV.

She'd tried her hardest to give him respite from his job. However, all the love, hugs, kisses and sex were nothing more than a distraction before he returned to crunching his thoughts.

Scott stared at the half-eaten bacon sandwich on his desk; for some reason his appetite was evading him. He had placed two calls to the forensics lab chasing DNA results, and they were chasing on his behalf. His inbox occupied his thoughts as he waited in desperation for an email to pop up.

Helen poked her head round the door, and Scott waved her in.

"I went to see Jackie Cartwright again, guv, and we went over her statement. We freewheeled about Linda's life, but I drew a blank." Helen shook her head.

"Nothing new?"

"She had nothing new to add. Linda was a complex character, with a complex love life. The only thing she did say was that a part of Linda wanted to be in love and have a normal happy family life, but then there was another part of her, almost her alter ego, that craved kinky sex."

It was the same conclusion he had arrived at during the night.

"Do you want me to tackle Linda's mum again, guv? I could –"

An email popped into his inbox. Scott flipped his hand up to stop Helen.

He couldn't click the mouse quick enough to open the body of the email. He scanned through the feedback. There was a negative match between Dalca's DNA and the samples recovered from Linda's body.

He read on.

"Fuck, fuck!" he shouted, standing abruptly. His chair flew back and hit the wall.

Helen's eyes widened in consternation, searching Scott for an answer. He beckoned her through to the main floor.

"Richards!" he shouted. "He's our man."

The news startled the team. Mike, Abby and Raj spun round in their chairs, stopping what they were doing.

"Forensics has just come back. Dalca is negative. Richards is positive. His DNA profile matches the semen sample profile retrieved from Linda's body. And...he's a match for Daisy Callaghan."

The news had the team exchanging glances, as the pieces fell in place.

"Wait...wait," Abby said. She pressed her fingers to her temples and closed her eyes. Her mind raced at warp speed through the memories of the past few weeks. Something clearly prickled her awareness. Was it something she had heard? Was it something she had seen?

All eyes were locked on Abby.

Silence followed.

Scott couldn't bear the wait. "What?"

Abby shook her head and waved her hands at him. "I don't know. Something I've seen, but I can't place it."

Raj said, "Guv, Richards made it very clear he didn't think much of Linda. That being the case, why would Linda get in the car with him? She knew he was dangerous, and he was the last person she would want to be with."

Scott paced the floor as he joined the dots together. "That's true, Raj. But Richards could have set up a fake profile to lure Linda into believing that the profile was genuine. When we went to Richards's house, I noticed several mobile phones in the lounge. My guess is he used one to communicate with Linda and Daisy. That's why Richards's number never appeared in the call log we pulled off her phone."

"So, when Richards turned up at the pub and the penny dropped, she left the same time as him?" Raj suggested.

Scott nodded. And from there, it would have been easy for Richards to bundle her into his car.

"Abby, get a warrant for Richards's arrest, and a search of his apartment. And make it quick," Scott ordered.

Abby spun round in her chair and grabbed her phone in one deft move.

"Mike, put SOCO on standby. Arrange for a dog handler, because Richards has a Staffordshire bull terrier, and get the tactical entry team to meet us at his property. We need to find him, and fast."

The team jumped to their feet, grabbing jackets, and utility belts. A buzz of excitement rippled through them. Investigating a crime was a large part of their job, but catching the perp was why they put in the time, effort, and energy.

Scott had suspected that Richards was their key suspect, but he'd had to be patient to gather the evidence to confirm his hunch.

The team's arrival drew attention. Curtains twitched in surrounding properties. The odd neighbour found a pressing need to retrieve something from their car, or anything that would give them a clearer vantage point. Nosey neighbours were a hazard of the job.

With two unmarked cars, a police carrier with eight officers, a local dog unit, and a white scientific services van at the tail, the law enforcement convoy was anything but discreet. The team piled out and gathered around Scott for final instructions before they dispersed and took up positions.

With the hallway outside Richards's apartment crammed with officers, and several others positioned outside covering the perimeter, Scott hammered on the door several times and announced himself. He placed his ear to the wood to pick up on any sounds. After several minutes and repeated attempts, Scott gave the nod, and a large, uniformed officer dressed in protective body armour stepped forward. He held the red key, used by the tactical entry team to gain access to properties.

The officer drew it back before thrusting it at the lock in the door. The door shook in its frame but held firm. The surrounding walls rumbled from the shock waves. The officer pulled back and attempted re-entry several times, before the door relented and flew in, crashing against the wall. Fragments of wood splintered, and the projectiles scattered in all directions.

"Police stay where you are. Police!" shouted the first few officers that piled through the door, protected by heavy-duty gloves, shields, and reinforced overalls. The dog handler followed in behind them, a dog pole in one hand. He was followed by another uniformed officer with a fire extinguisher.

With the dog under control and having been removed from the apartment, officers began their search of the property. It was just as untidy, smelly and neglected as Scott's first visit. It disappointed him to not find Richards. On a Monday morning, he'd hoped Richards would be fast asleep, nursing a hangover from the night before. But with him out of the way, they could take the place apart.

The mobile phones Scott had seen on their previous visit hadn't been moved, and they were the first things to be bagged up in clear evidence bags.

"Guv, over here," Mike shouted from the kitchen. Scott walked through to find Mike holding several clear plastic bags, and duct tape. "Could be the same as those used on Linda."

"Possibly. Leave them on the table and let SOCO have a look."

Scott walked around the property; he peered into cupboards, pulled out drawers, and looked behind sofas. There was nothing to begin with that linked Richards to the crime, but an officer discovered a folded piece of paper tucked away in a jacket buried deep in one cupboard. Information on the paper suggested they had hit the jackpot.

It was a list of female names, with their online usernames written in brackets. To anyone, it could have been a random list of names, but what piqued Scott's interest was the fact that Linda Allen's name was on it, together with the username she'd used on the adult contact sites. This was the second crucial piece of information tying Richards to the murder of Linda Allen.

Scott, Abby and Mike congregated in the lounge, whilst officers busied themselves going through Richards's clothes, looking under rugs, and examining everything that might link him to the crime. Car keys belonging to Richards had been found, and an officer was sent outside to locate the vehicle.

"It will be worth checking those names against the mis per list," Abby remarked, as she looked around the room.

Scott agreed. The first name he checked was Rebecca Levy. Thankfully, her name wasn't on there, but that didn't rule Richards out from being involved in her disappearance. The list could have been compiled after Rebecca's disappearance, the list could be incomplete, or he may have deliberately left her name off the list.

It was whilst Abby glanced around the room that she stopped, her thoughts whirring. Then it hit like a steam train. The thing she couldn't remember earlier. She moved swiftly over to a series of photo frames she had cast an eye over on their last visit. She scanned each one before grabbing one, a picture of Richards standing amongst others, their pint glasses raised. It wasn't the picture that interested Abby but the date stamp in the bottom right-hand corner.

She pulled the photo in for closer inspection. "I knew it. Fucking knew it." She walked over to Mike and Scott and held it out for them to see.

"The day that Daisy Callaghan was murdered." Scott raised a brow and glanced at Abby, who nodded furiously.

She said, "We've got DNA evidence linking him to her murder, and we've got photographic evidence to prove he was in Cardiff that night...on a stag weekend."

33

The search of Richard's the apartment had continued into the evening. Further evidence had been bagged up, documented and transported to the station for closer examination. The occasional neighbour had stopped by to ask the uniformed officer on guard what had happened, but received nothing more than a cursory dismissal.

Whilst forensics picked their way through the evidence at the scene, it had given Scott, Abby and Mike the chance to grab a light bite nearby.

"I'm bloody famished," Mike protested, as he tried to squeeze half a sandwich into his mouth.

"You can be so flipping gross sometimes, Mike," Abby said. She turned to look the opposite way as she ate her own.

"Well, we're tight on time, so I may as well eat as much as I can in case we don't get home till late."

Abby said, "I've got no problem with that. But when the guv said eat as much as you can, he didn't mean in one mouthful, you prat."

Mike tutted. "At least I eat. You live on bowls of cereal. And when you push out the boat and have something half decent, you have a bloody boiled egg for lunch. And nothing else. What's all that about?"

Abby took the bait every time Mike teased her. "You can be such a dick sometimes. What I eat is none of your business."

"They should arrest you for crimes against food. Wilful neglect of food."

Abby scrunched up a napkin and threw it at Mike's face.

Scott interrupted. "You two kids behave yourself or you'll both get detention – or in our case, the late shift."

The pair stared each other down, neither wishing to look away first.

"Our main concern is to find Richards," Scott added. "The uniformed patrols are scouring the streets, checking the local pubs, and tracking down all his known associates."

"Do you think he's gone to ground?" Mike asked.

"I hope not. But I'd much prefer that option than know he's with another victim."

The thought silenced all three.

BACK IN CID the team gathered, following further developments at the apartment.

Scott said, "They've located Richards's car. Forensics are poring over it downstairs. The search team found an unidentified key on his fob. We believe it's the type of key that might fit a lock on a safe deposit box, but they found none."

"Could it be stashed elsewhere?"

"Maybe, Raj. Richards did the odd gardening job, but no

gardening tools were discovered at his apartment or in his car. There was a pair of muddy boots in a carrier bag in the boot of his car."

"So that means he used his customer's tools?"

"Doubt that," Abby said. "I can't imagine any gardener turning up at a job without their own tools..."

"A lock-up then?" Raj speculated.

Scott nodded. "It would fit the type of key. Get in touch with the council and find out which garage units they rent out close to the station."

Raj glanced at his watch. "Guv, it's gone seven p.m. I doubt anyone's around."

"Use your nous. They'll have a twenty-four-hour emergency line. Phone around and tell whoever you speak to that we're in the middle of a murder investigation."

Raj nodded sheepishly as he spun round in his chair and searched online for a number.

Scott continued. "The search team have uncovered evidence that might be crucial for our investigation, and other mis per cases. They discovered a small silver necklace in the pocket of a pair of jeans. There might be a hair fibre caught in the links." He reviewed his notes. "And they also found underwear hidden in a carrier bag in the cupboard under his sink. Namely, two pairs of female knickers, a bra – oh, and a denim skirt."

The extent of the find wasn't lost on the team. If Richards's DNA was found on those items, then it pointed to the possibility that Richards was a serial rapist and murderer.

Abby turned to Helen. "Can you phone Claire Allen? It's a bit of a long shot, but considering Richards was once her son-in-law, she may know of places where he hung out, or know of other friends and associates that we may not be aware of."

Scott nodded in agreement. They had to exhaust every avenue of enquiry. He left the team to carry on whilst he went in search of Meadows. Scott knew it was easier to find the DS than have Meadows track him down in his brash and often aggressive manner.

MEADOWS SHIFTED paperwork around his desk, and tidied it into neat piles. All the corners matched up, and they sat angular with everything else on his desk. He was one of those people who forever extolled the virtues of a tidy desk equalling a tidy mind. Meadows preferred everything to be perfect before he left every evening. He would push his chair under the desk and pull his window blind up or down, but never halfway. His wastepaper basket would be by his door, ready for the evening cleaner, and any folders or reference books used during the day, would be returned to their rightful place.

Scott tapped on the open door twice and lingered in the doorway.

DS Meadows looked up at him. "Ah, Scott, I was looking for you earlier."

Scott doubted that. He had been in for a while now and hadn't seen Meadows.

The DS said, "It looks like we've got our man from what I'm hearing?"

Scott nodded. "It looks like that, sir. On the face of it, we have enough evidence linking him to the rape and murder of two women. The Cardiff boys will be pleased that their case has been solved, which is a bonus."

"And not so pleased that we've got the suspect and solved their case for them." Meadows offered the slightest smile.

"Well, we haven't got him yet. He was gone when we executed a search warrant. We've got officers looking for him. If we move quickly, I'm hoping for an arrest in the next twelve- to twenty-four hours."

Meadows scrunched his eyes in displeasure. "Jesus, Scott, if we wait that long, he could be halfway across the country."

"That is a risk, sir. But we have his car. I'm hoping that will slow him down. I've got an officer stationed outside his apartment in case he comes back."

Meadows stuffed papers into his briefcase, not wishing to stay later than he needed to. "Contact the media team, Scott. Circulate his face to social media and the press this evening. That might smoke him out and force him into making a mistake. I suggest we put out the usual statement. Something like, 'We are keen to speak to John Richards. We believe he may be able to help us in an ongoing investigation regarding the sexual assault and murder of a woman from Brighton a week ago. We advise the public not to approach him if seen, but to contact the police immediately.' That should do it."

"I'll get onto that right away, sir."

Meadows rose and grabbed his suit jacket. "Good man. If there are any problems, then call me. But *only* if it's an emergency. I'm going to the theatre tonight, so I will have my phone on silent."

That was Meadows's code for "he did not want to be disturbed."

THE MEDIA TEAM swung into action and within thirty minutes of Scott leaving Meadows, Richards's face was splashed across the Facebook pages of the Brighton and Hove police, *The Argus* and BBC Sussex.

With Raj and Helen covering the late shift, it was now a waiting game whilst the net closed in on Richards.

Scott took the opportunity to spend quality time with Cara. He had neglected her recently and knew she felt the same way. He'd stopped at Sainsbury's to pick up a bunch of flowers. At that time of night few places were open, so choice was limited. He loitered in the wine aisle, undecided on which bottle to pick. He must have picked up over a dozen bottles and studied the labels. The descriptions baffled him. He was anything but a wine connoisseur – bouquet this, floral that, buttery characteristics, cream-like textures. He shook his head in consternation. Flamboyant, toasty, charcoal, bright, rustic, complex, dense, earthy. It amused him to think someone had been paid to come up with these descriptions.

He chose a Chilean red wine. Cabernet Sauvignon. He recalled an elderly neighbour he'd once lived next door to. A gentleman in his seventies, Jack had a full head of hair, white as snow, and only had Chilean red wine. Scott had popped in to check up on him, as he did every week. Jack had asked Scott to join him in a glass. After that night, Scott had become a convert. It was the only red wine he would touch.

He picked up a microwave meal to go with it.

Cara was at home, wrapped in her fluffy dressing gown, tucked into a corner of the sofa, with her feet underneath her, and a steaming mug of tea cradled in both hands.

She glanced up when she heard the front door open, and waited. Her face lit up on seeing Scott walk in.

Scott bent over her and planted a soft kiss on her lips.

"These are for you," he said, handing her the flowers.

She cooed in delight. "You shouldn't have. What's the occasion?"

"Do I need an occasion to buy my girlfriend some flowers and treat her to a bottle of wine?" he replied, holding up the bottle.

"Of course not. They're lovely, thank you." She lifted the bunch and buried her nose in the petals.

"I've bought dinner, too. I hope you haven't eaten. It's boeuf bourguignon, your favourite."

Cara got up and made her way around to Scott. Her feet padded lightly on the floor. "I feel underdressed," she said, glancing down.

Scott wrapped his arms around her waist. "You look beautiful as you are. Just perfect for dinner. Besides, it won't be on for long," he said, tugging on her collar.

Cara noticed the glint in Scott's eye. Her stomach flipped and her heart fluttered. She ached inside for him. Just the sight of her man was enough to turn her on. As she headed to the kitchen, she couldn't wait to get dinner out of the way.

Scott grabbed her arm as she passed him. He pulled her in close, kissing her deeply. Their tongues explored each other; their bodies pressed together as one.

"I know I've been busy at work," Scott said, "and I'm sorry if you've felt I've been neglecting you, but you're never far from my thoughts. And even though I haven't been around much and maybe a bit distant, I would swap all of that for moments like this."

Cara's dark-brown eyes gushed with love and happiness as she stared at Scott for what seemed an eternity. Their eyes explored, connected, and spoke silently. She pulled Scott in again and kissed him once more.

34

The low hum of vibration stirred Scott. It sounded like a mosquito buzzing near his ear, or a bee in flight. Maybe he was dreaming and it was his subconscious stirring. He rolled over to get away from the noise. But it persisted, gnawing at his awareness.

As he rolled back the other way, his body became trapped in the duvet cover. Somewhere deep within his mind alarm bells rang, shaking him from a comatose state.

One eye cracked open, drawn to the light that flashed by his side of the bed.

Shit!

Scott jerked upright and swung his legs over the side of the bed. He grabbed his phone as the buzzing grew louder.

"Yesss..."

"Guv, sorry to wake you, but we've had a report come in of an attempted abduction." It was Raj.

Scott rubbed his eyes. His mind somersaulted as he tried to pull himself into consciousness. "Details, Raj."

"Female aged twenty-seven. She was walking back from

town and noticed a man following her. She sped up, and he did too. Whilst fumbling for her phone, she dropped it. In the end she ran for it, and he pursued her. The suspect caught her, pulled a carrier bag over her head, and tightened it around her throat. He proceeded to put his hand up her skirt and sexually assault her. He tried to haul her off towards some parked cars. Luckily for her, she fought back. The assailant ran off."

"Description of the man?"

"IC1 male. Medium height and overweight. A stubbly beard, with heavy jowls, and she said he smelt of fags. He didn't try to hide his face."

"Are uniform on the ground?"

"Yes, guv. They're doing a sweep of the area. The victim is in hospital being treated for minor injuries and shock."

"Where did the attack take place?"

"Two streets away from The Greys Pub."

SCOTT WAS BACK in the office by three a.m. He sat with Raj and Helen, reviewing the incident report, a large, strong cup of black coffee by his side. He wiped his bleary eyes.

The unpredictability of the job often led to situations where the senior officer would be called in at short notice or on his rest days, to deal with an ongoing situation.

"Do you think it's Richards?" Raj said.

Scott shrugged. "It could be Richards, considering the location and the nature of the attack."

Helen agreed as she looked at the incident board; Richards and his smug grin stared back at her. With the attack taking place so close to where Linda Allen had been last seen, it wasn't uncommon for an assailant to return to an area they were familiar with.

"The victim was on a night out with friends," Helen said. "The circumstances of the attack are different in relation to Linda's abduction and murder. Could that suggest Richards is getting desperate?"

"Desperate and dangerous," Scott said.

"Do you want me to call in Mike and Abby?" Helen asked.

"Call Mike in. Abby is not due in until ten a.m. Let her stick to that." Scott had promised Abby a better work life balance. Although he needed her in, he would make do with the resources he had. The rest of the team were more than capable to progress the investigation.

Raj said, "I managed to get through to someone in the council regarding garages they rent out. It turns out they have close to one hundred sites across Brighton and Hove, from Woodingdean in the east to Portslade in the west."

"All occupied?" Scott asked Raj.

"Not all of them, guv. Some are vacant, and others have a waiting list. None of the occupied garages tally with Richards's name. So that leaves more than forty sites that still have space. That's far too many for us to cover with the time that we have."

Scott walked around the CID floor weighing up his next move. Richards was out there. He was a creature of habit, and if they linked tonight's assault to him, then it confirmed suspicions that Richards was still in Brighton.

"Any word on the street?" Scott asked.

"We spoke to his known associates and we've contacted our informants," said Raj. "No one has seen him."

Scott turned to Helen. "Did you get in touch with Claire Allen?"

"I did. She didn't know where he might be. And as she put it, 'she couldn't give a fuck where he was, hopefully in a body bag,' so I think he's off her Christmas card list." Helen sighed.

Scott knew they were running out of options. They needed to move fast. There were a few avenues they could follow.

Scott grabbed the nearest chair and sat down next to Helen. "Get onto Richards's mobile phone company. See if they can get a triangulation for us, ASAP. If his phone is on or has been used recently, then that will help us narrow down the search area."

"I thought we retrieved several phones during the search of his apartment?" Helen asked.

"We did. But that's not to say he didn't have more. Raj, get back on to your contact at the council. Ask them to cross-reference Richards's name with past records. Tell them it's a matter of urgency."

Raj had already picked up the phone and was tapping in the numbers before Scott finished his sentence.

Scott needed DNA evidence from the assault victim, which would have been obtained in the hospital. Scrapings would have been taken from beneath her nails, and her clothes would have been kept for evidence. But it would be hours before he received confirmation.

The waiting game was a skill that every officer had to be familiar with. Whether it was waiting for a suspect to turn up at a location, or waiting for the results of forensic analysis, or even waiting on an answer from CPS, many hours and days could be lost. Scott found it the most frustrating part of his job.

He left Helen and Raj to follow through with their enquiries, whilst he visited the scene of the latest assault.

NEWARK PLACE SAT in an elevated position several streets away from where Linda Allen had last been seen. It was a tight and narrow street. On one side sat a row of featureless, flat-fronted terraced housing that looked narrow in proportion. Scott imagined they were two-up two-down residences. Ideal as student lets. The other side was a long brick wall that marked the boundary for gardens belonging to houses in the next street.

Police officers had cordoned off the area where the assault had taken place and had completed their fingertip search. Two patrol cars blocked either end of the street, and half a dozen police officers were compiling their notes following door-to-door enquiries.

Scott looked at the darkened street. It offered an ideal location for a predator to stalk a victim and launch an attack. With houses on one side of the street only, it halved the opportunity to be discovered or seen. What Scott found most alarming was the lack of street lighting, providing opportunity for someone to lurk in the shadows behind cars, waiting to pounce.

He picked his location well, Scott thought. He glanced up and down the street. *There is nowhere for a victim to run.*

A uniformed officer approached him. "Guv, we've completed our enquiries here. Is there anything else you need us to do?"

Scott stuffed his hands in his pockets. The cold night air crept through the fibres in his clothes and tickled his skin. Shivers raced down his spine. "Did anything get thrown up in the witness statements?"

The officer shook his head. He went on to explain that several residents did venture out but only saw a man from behind disappear around the corner at the far end of the street.

The officer left Scott alone with his thoughts. If this was Richards, he was both brazen and desperate. His need to stalk women and attack them, despite the inherent danger. It suggested this was an addictive behaviour that needed feeding.

As Scott walked back to his car, his phone vibrated in his pocket. It was Helen.

"Guv, I think we've got him. The triangulation gave us a hit near to you. And better still, Raj has been on to the council. Richards rented a garage for about five years. He didn't renew his contract when it ended three months ago. And check this out. The garage is still available for rent, and it's in the vicinity of the triangulation."

35

The team, together with backup, arrived at a row of six garages a few hundred yards behind Brighton rail station. The units were tucked away in a small residential street. Each metal garage door was painted green. Several were in use, as the paint was clean and well looked after. Two units appeared to not have been in use for some time. Cobwebs crept down from the brickwork over peeling and faded paint.

It was still dark and just after six a.m. Brighton was waking, as commuters made their way to the train station. The increased police activity caused many to cast a secondary glance as they hurried, keen to avoid missing their train.

Mike and Helen had joined Scott. Raj held back in the office and continued with his research. A half-dozen other uniformed officers joined the group, fanning out along the row of garages, standing in readiness.

Uncertainty plagued Scott, but he hoped evidence linked

to Richards would be discovered in the garage. Richards may have kept a copy of the key or broken in knowing it was empty. It would provide a perfect escape bolthole.

They had approached the garage in silence, not wishing to disturb Richards if he was there. Scott had tried the lock and found it to be shut. He tried the key that Helen had brought with her from Richards's key fob. It fitted the style of the door lock but didn't turn. Expecting that possibility, he had called ahead for a locksmith who approached the lock with a sizeable cordless drill.

With all the officers positioned and ready to storm the unit, Scott gave the locksmith a nod. The man was thickset and heavily overweight. He leant his weight behind the drill as he positioned the bit in the slot. A high-pitched, metallic whirring shrill broke the silence.

The anticipation was a nervous energy. It tingled through Scott like electrical sparks on the way to the ground, gathering in his toes. He curled his fingers around his Maglite torch and glanced across to Mike, who was giving the door a stone-cold stare. Helen stood beside Mike, ready to move. Courage oozed from her. She would be the first to storm in when given the chance.

The other uniformed officers readied themselves; several held torches, others held their batons in readiness, all unsure what to expect. A risk assessment had been undertaken enroute to the location. Information suggested that Richards, although violent, didn't carry a threat in relation to carrying a firearm or other deadly weapon.

The locksmith twisted the handle to release the broken lock. He stepped back a few paces and hid behind the safety of the officers gathered, wariness etched on his face, concern narrowing his eyes.

Scott braced himself. Tension rippled in the air. It snapped and crackled like electricity that ran along the power lines and fizzed on rainy days.

A uniformed officer pulled the door up and over his head as his colleagues surged in.

"Police stay where you are!" they shouted in unison.

They ground to a halt a few feet in the doorway. Scott pushed through them and stared into the darkened space, lit only by the glare from white pulses of light. "Fuck."

"Bollocks," Mike returned.

As adrenaline left Scott's body, a thick silence enveloped them all. They stared in disbelief and disappointment at the empty garage. It had been stripped clean. Cobwebs hung from the ceiling, and the floor was dusty and oily. The unit hadn't been used in ages.

They stepped out into the darkened driveway and glanced around.

Helen sighed. "I thought we had him, guv."

"So did I. The triangulation shows that the phone's location is nearby. The stats only give us a broad area from which to work, and we're looking at an area of around a few hundred yards in radius, maybe more. He could be holed up in any house around here." There was disappointment and frustration in Scott's tone.

He pulled out his phone and called Raj.

On the third ring he answered. "Raj, we drew a blank. The garage was empty. But if he is with his phone, then he's nearby. Has anything come through from the press release?"

The line went silent whilst Raj checked online. "No confirmed sighting, guv. We had a few calls suggesting he looked familiar, but nothing concrete. I've got a few more to go through."

Scott thought for a few seconds, a mixture of frustration, anger and embarrassment flashing through him. It felt like they were clutching at straws and chasing their tails. Relying on nothing more than phone triangulation didn't fill him with positivity. There was the chance that the phone had been discarded.

"Raj, do me a favour. Can you get onto the phone company and ask for a new triangulation? Just in case they've got it wrong."

An anxious wait followed as officers mingled around their cars. Helen and one other officer had gone in search of refreshments and had come back with a tray of hot drinks and some croissants.

Scott knew relying on cell site triangulation carried risks. In built-up urban areas, the triangulation was more accurate due to closer proximity of mobile masts. In Brighton, most masts were closer to the city centre. The problem Scott considered was that if one mast was busy, the signal would ping off the next available mast. That would distort the results and skew the triangulation.

Mike, Helen and Scott sat in silence. Mike burped, much to Helen's annoyance.

"Do you think there are more vics out there?" he asked of no one as he stared out of the window.

"I suspect there are," Scott said. "Now we have his DNA, we can do a nationwide database check. I wouldn't be surprised if there are more victims who survived but didn't come forward..."

"Or victims who didn't survive and may never be found," Mike added.

Scott knew that more than eighty percent of victims

never reported a sexual assault to police. With more than an estimated five hundred thousand victims a year, many assailants got away with their crimes.

Scott's phone rang and startled all three. It was Raj.

"Guv, I've checked the triangulation area again, and nothing's changed. Within the identified area, there's another group of four garages owned by the council. Three are occupied. The fourth is empty."

Scott nodded at Mike, giving him the signal to start the car and notify the police carrier parked in front. They moved off as Raj provided them with the address about half a mile away. Raj called again when they were less than a few minutes away.

"Guv, I'm going through more calls from the press release. A member of the public believes they recognised Richards's picture. The caller returned late from work, and as she exited the car, saw a man matching Richards's description walk past. She described the character as acting suspiciously. The man kept looking over his shoulder, was walking in a hurry, with his hands tucked in his pockets, and had a baseball cap pulled low over his eyes."

The description excited Scott. What made the sighting crucial was the witness lived less than one hundred yards away from the garages they were heading to.

They gathered outside the second garage. Scott checked the edges of the door. There were no cobwebs that would suggest a lack of use. There were fresh scrapings on the floor from where one corner of the door had caught the floor each time it was opened.

Scott tried the key in the lock. He paused when it turned and unlocked the handle. The locksmith breathed a sigh of relief. He took a few steps back and positioned himself a safe distance behind the row of police officers.

Scott stepped aside as a burly police officer grabbed the handle and yanked on the door. It didn't move. The officer tugged again, but the door refused to budge.

"We need to get this open," Scott whispered, realising that the door must be secured from the inside somehow. It heightened his expectation that this was the garage they were looking for.

Two other police officers stepped forward with large crowbars and wedged them into either side of the door. The metal bent and creaked under the pressure. Other officers joined in as they grabbed at the edges. Some minutes later the door relented, as mechanisms behind it snapped and cracked, causing it to fly open.

A wave of uniforms flooded in. With enough natural daylight, there was less of a need for torches.

"Police! Stay where you are!" they shouted en masse.

In comparison to the last empty garage, this one contained brown storage boxes stacked haphazardly to one side. Garden implements, a wheelbarrow, plus other assorted tools were scattered around the spare space. The far end of the garage was stacked floor to ceiling with more cardboard boxes, which reduced the length of space in the garage by half. There were far too many officers in the limited space available, so several stepped out.

There were mixed feelings amongst the team. A natural disappointment at not finding Richards, but the tools and boxes more than likely belonged to him. The officers would be on site for some hours as they meticulously assessed and documented everything found.

As the officers spoke amongst themselves, Scott took a moment to reflect by the edge of the garage. Confusion and suspicion gnawed away at him. Triangulation details put Richards, or at least his phone, in the vicinity, and Scott was in possession of the key to this garage. He stepped back into the gloom of the garage and walked amongst the boxes. He scanned one then another, hoping that something would jump out of him.

Scott sighed and turned. He had only walked a few steps when he halted. A noise was coming from behind him. His eyes darted from left to right as he tuned in to the sound. He stared at the wall of boxes.

Mice? Rats? More than likely.

Scott stepped forward and pressed his ear against the boxes. He searched for the noise again, but conversations from outside made it harder. He clicked his fingers a few times to get the officers' attention and placed a finger to his lips. The conversations dulled as officers turned to face him.

Scott listened again. Nothing. Then he heard it again. A slight shuffling. Silence. More shuffling.

Taking a step back, Scott signalled for the officers to join him. And in silence, they formed a human chain, removing one box after another. A partitioned wall started to reveal itself, with an improvised door made of OSB board fixed by long, black hinges.

"This is the police, open up!" Scott shouted, as he hammered on the door.

The sound from inside became frenetic. The shuffling increased. He stepped back and turned to the nearest officer dressed in protective gear and gave him the nod. The officer swung at the door with the red enforcer. The wall shuddered under the impact, and after a few thrusts, the board shattered.

"Open!" ordered Scott, as he stood out of the way. "Now! Get the bloody thing open."

He watched as the officers forced their way in. Whoever was in there was cornered, and Scott had no idea who lurked in the darkness, or how they would react.

Other officers joined as they grabbed the edges and pulled the door off its hinges. "Police!" yelled the officers, as they prepared to surge through the gap they had made in the wall.

A figure charged towards them from the darkness beyond. With a hammer in one hand, he raced towards the nearest officer, his lips pulled back and snarling like a rabid dog.

The hammer connected with the officer's shoulder, sending him to the floor howling in pain.

The crazy man swung wildly as other officers surrounded him, each one ducking from the arc of each swing. If it hadn't have been such a dangerous situation, the scene would have been comical, as officers stumbled out of the way and fell over the array of boxes that lay scattered across the floor.

One officer pulled out her Taser and took aim, just as Mike charged forward and went in low to rugby-tackle the assailant from the front. Scott raced in from behind. Between them, they brought the large man down to the ground, and grappled with him on the floor. Mike's large frame smothered the man, as Scott tussled with the hand that tried to wildly swing the hammer.

More officers joined in. They pinned the man down by

his legs before flipping him onto his front and applying cuffs from behind.

The torchlight from one officer illuminated the man's face. As the body slumped in defeat, Scott let out a long breath he must have been holding for ages.

It was Richards.

36

Scott scanned the room minutes after Richards's arrest. It was nothing more than an improvised bolt-hole that smelt of stale sweat and general mustiness, due to a lack of proper ventilation. Empty cans of beer lay strewn in one corner and half a packet of custard creams, together with a torch were on top of a box. A scrunched up sleeping bag had been pushed to one side. Scott snapped on a pair of latex gloves and examined carrier bags discarded in one corner. The illumination from a torch that Mike held lit up the darkened space.

"He's kicking up a right fuss out there. I've let Helen deal with it, because if he pisses me off any more, I might just batter him with this torch." Mike grunted his displeasure.

"It's hardly an ensuite, is it?" Scott said, as he rummaged through the first bag. "Bingo." He pulled out an assortment of women's underwear. In a second bag, he discovered women's shoes and other items of clothing.

He turned in anger and exited the room, instructing Mike to arrange for scientific services to review the evidence.

Scott glared at Richards. "Who do all those items of clothing and shoes belong to?" He flicked his head in the direction of the garage.

Richards offered nothing more than a demented grin.

He inched closer to Richards. "If I find that those items in there belong to other victims, I'll make sure you're banged up for a long time."

Richards spat at him and tried to wriggle free of the police officers.

"Get a fucking spit hood on this animal." Scott grabbed Richards by his top. "Who else have you attacked? Who?"

"Guv!" Helen shouted.

Scott almost didn't hear her. He was lost in rage-fuelled anger. This case had consumed him. And having seen the evidence, he suspected that Linda Allen had been one of Richards's many victims.

His grip tightened on Richards. Scott leant in closer and whispered, "I will make your last hours of freedom so fucking miserable for you that you will wish you'd never been born."

Helen placed a hand on Scott's arm and tugged him away. "Guv, enough!" she said firmly.

Richards offered nothing more than a stare filled with pure hatred.

"I CAN'T BELIEVE you didn't call me in," Abby fumed, as she looked at the monitor of an adjoining room where Richards was sitting, in a white suit. She felt cheated, having missed out on the final few hours of tracking down the killer.

Scott shrugged. "I didn't get the chance," he lied. "Things

happened so quickly that I barely had enough time to call Mike."

Abby eyed Scott. "You're a lousy liar, guv."

Forensics had uncovered hair fibres from the impounded car. Some fibres matched Linda Allen. Other hair fibres extracted were being referenced against the mis per list. Analysis was taking place on the soil samples taken from work boots discovered in the boot of the car.

It was clear from the start of the interview that Richards would not cooperate. Scott had tried every form of coercion and pressure, going in soft and then hard, but nothing worked. Richards sat back in his chair, his arms folded defiantly, refusing to talk. They had appointed a duty solicitor who had little work to do, as her client answered every question with a "no comment" that tested Scott's patience.

But the file of evidence they had against Richards was substantial, and they presented each piece of evidence to gauge his reaction. His DNA matched the DNA profile from semen taken from Linda Allen and Daisy Callaghan. The black pubic hair retrieved from Linda Allen during the post-mortem matched Richards's profile. The bags and duct tape found in his house matched the same composition of those discovered on Linda. And finally, the photograph taken in Cardiff confirmed he'd been there the night Daisy Callaghan was murdered. It was all they needed.

Abby and Scott stared at the monitor as Richards locked his gaze on the camera in the corner of the ceiling, and gave it a finger salute. Scott turned to Abby, who looked as frustrated as Scott felt. Not every arrest ended with a full and frank confession during the interview. And in such cases, Scott would charge the offender based on evidence that linked them to the crime and hoped CPS would agree.

But Scott wanted to give it one more attempt.

Seated before Richards once again, Abby joined Scott, not wishing to miss out.

Scott held up another clear evidence bag that contained the list of female names recovered from the apartment. Shelly Martin and Zoe Evans on the list had been found safe and well. They had not been contacted by Richards directly, but he'd liked their profiles and sent them virtual gifts. They hadn't been able to locate a female called Katrina Banis yet.

"Laura Winters, missing for the past two years. Did you have anything to do with her disappearance?" Scott asked.

Richards shook his head.

"For the purpose of the tape, could you say your answers, Mr Richards?"

Richards threw Scott a derisory glance. "No."

Scott sighed. "Anahit Grigoryan, she arrived in the UK six months ago from Armenia. She went missing three months after her arrival. Did you have anything to do with her disappearance?"

"Nope."

"Emma Ali. Reported missing ten days ago. Did you have anything to do with her disappearance?"

"No comment."

The interview turned into a battle of wills. It was evident that Richards would stonewall Scott's questions. Scott hoped the underwear, clothing and shoes discovered at the garage and apartment would yield forensic evidence linking Richards to those missing females in the coming hours and days.

He slid a picture of Linda across the table. "She was your wife at one point. What could be so horrible that would drive a man to kill his ex-wife?"

"No comment," Richards replied flatly, as he rocked on the back two legs of his chair.

Scott maintained the silence for a few minutes before removing another photograph from the Manila covered file. He pushed it in Richards's direction.

"The mother of *your* daughter. A child who has lost her mum. A mum who won't be there to see her daughter turn sweet sixteen, eighteen or twenty-one. Who won't be there to see her girl go to her school prom." Scott turned to Abby. "Can you imagine the psychological trauma Shannon will go through when she's old enough to realise that her dad killed her mum?"

Abby shook her head at the question and stared intently at Richards. There was no reaction. Richards was nothing more than a cold, calculated, psychotic killer who held no remorse.

Scott took another line of questioning. "Where was your last gardening job?"

Richards shrugged. "I can't remember."

"It must have been wet? It's covered your boots in mud, and some of it's still damp, so it must've been recent?"

"As I said, I can't remember."

"I imagine it upset you that Linda needed to go elsewhere to find love, romance and sex. Did it make you feel inadequate?"

Richards's eye muscle twitched, and Scott pounced. "What was it? Couldn't get it up? Not packing enough down there?"

Richards bristled further.

Scott went for the jugular. "Linda confided in her friends you weren't up to the job and was surprised as you were when she fell pregnant."

Anger boiled deep. It churned within, hungry for destruction. Richards lunged at Scott and sent the papers flying. The duty solicitor recoiled in horror as pandemonium broke out. Richards grappled with Scott's jacket just as Abby hit the dado panic strip. Richards shifted his grip and reached for Scott's throat.

Abby raced around the table and threw her arm around Richards's neck, trying to pull him back. Her restraint only enraged him further. Spittle erupted from his mouth and his face reddened in fury.

Officers piled into the room amid the wail of the emergency siren. Several manhandled Richards to the floor as he screamed vile obscenities. One sealed his fate.

"The bitch deserved it."

"You okay?" Abby asked Scott, a concerned look on her face.

Scott nodded and slumped in his chair. "Not the outcome I hoped for. The findings at the garage have come a little late to nail him today, but I'm hoping there's enough there to link him to some of those missing women."

Abby leant against the wall, a sense of anti-climax hanging heavily in the air. "The phones that we seized show he's been in contact with over a dozen women in the past twelve months. All the conversations relate to online meetings and sites. Some are still active and accounted for. Five have not been online in over three months. But that's not uncommon. Perhaps they met someone, or their membership has expired. We'll follow up with further enquiries."

"At least we've charged him with the murders of Linda Allen and Daisy Callaghan," Scott said.

It was a good outcome for the team. But one name still concerned him. Rebecca Levy.

Not knowing her fate played heavily on Scott's mind. With nothing to suggest that she'd come to harm, he could only guess that she was one of the many who had disappeared for reasons only known to them. Maybe they would never uncover new information about her disappearance.

Scott couldn't help but feel for Mr Levy. He was one of thousands of parents each year living for news of missing loved ones. They lived in hope, and for many, hope was the only thing that kept them going.

37

NINE WEEKS LATER...

"It must be around here somewhere!" Adam shouted.

The three of them stopped and examined the map, familiarising themselves with their surroundings. Whichever direction they looked, the woodland appeared the same.

"I think we're not far. We've been on this trail for over an hour already," Stevie added with enthusiasm. He was the persistent one of the three, and the first to look up new sites to uncover. Adam and Dean followed his lead.

Together, they'd researched, discovered, broken into and explored dozens of abandoned hospitals, building sites, mortuaries and properties off limits to the public. They were part of a growing movement of urban explorers who travelled the length and breadth of the country searching out weird, unusual, and sometimes scary locations. Once inside, they'd explore, take photos and upload their experiences online.

They'd already been to Draycott Cross Colliery in Derbyshire, GKN Shadow Factory tunnels in Smethwick, St

Peter's Hospital Mortuary based in Chertsey, and the old cement works at Shoreham. They'd evaded security and barbed wire at many of these sites.

Their new site for exploration was the abandoned underground reservoir in Plumpton, north of Brighton. Surrounded by dense woodland and deep undergrowth, their journey was slow and hard as the ground was wet underfoot.

Some thirty minutes later, they knew they were close when rusty and broken metal railings loomed into view.

Excitement and a sense of curiosity filled their veins as they examined the site. At ground level there was little to see. In fact, the location looked no different to the rest of the forest. The magic lay beneath their feet. Several explorers had posted their photos of the underground cavern. Dark, decaying walls, and a chamber partly submerged.

They split in different directions to search the ground.

It didn't take long for Dean to discover the grate. "Here lads, I've found it, I think."

The other two joined him. On first impression, it looked like nothing more than a rusty floor grate in the ground hidden by fallen leaves. Fresh footprints suggested that other explorers had recently visited. The discovery of a torch nearby only reinforced the assumption.

"Give us a hand." Dean huffed, as he gripped the cold steel and tugged with all his might. Together, the three pulled the grate to one side and peered over the edge into the blackness.

"You found it, so you go first," Adam suggested, readying his camera kit and headlamp.

By now their combat fatigues were muddy and wet. They

knelt on the sodden ground and watched Dean descend the metal stairs into the murky blackness.

His voice echoed around the narrow passage as the light from the headlamp bobbed and bounced off the walls.

"Jesus, it fucking stinks down here..." His voice trailed off. "Someone's been here; they've left clothes and a sleeping bag on the ledge."

Stevie and Adam exchanged excited glances and readied themselves to descend.

They stopped in their tracks when Dean's guttural scream raced up the inspection chamber.

"Call the police, call the police!" He screamed like a wounded animal. As he clambered up, his feet slipped on the wet rungs.

He scrambled up to the surface and dragged himself over the edge only to collapse on the wet ground. He threw up as his stomach lurched. His face was ashen. He lay on his back staring up at the sky. His chest heaved with shock.

His friends' voices became a distant echo as they crowded around him in concern. His brain had shut down. He was clammy, his skin glistening with cold sweat. His eyes were as wide as if someone was coming to deliver the fatal blow. Yet what he'd seen, the bodies... no one else should see.

Trapped in his own psychosis, Dean experienced a living nightmare for one, tailor-made by his own brain to play on his deepest fears.

WE HOPE YOU ENJOYED THIS BOOK

If you could spend a moment to write an honest review on Amazon, no matter how short, we would be extremely grateful. They really do help readers discover new authors.

ALSO BY JAY NADAL

TIME TO DIE

(Book 1 in the DI Scott Baker series)

THE STOLEN GIRLS

(Book 2 in the DI Scott Baker series)

ONE DEADLY LESSON

(Book 3 in the DI Scott Baker series)

IN PLAIN SIGHT

(Book 4 in the DI Scott Baker series)

AN EVIL OFFERING

(Book 5 in the DI Scott Baker series)

EYE FOR AN EYE

(Book 6 in the DI Scott Baker series)

MARKED FOR DEATH

(Book 7 in the DI Scott Baker series)

Made in the USA
Monee, IL
05 September 2023

42206696R00152